Summer Wine

ETHEL PAQUIN

Harlequin Books

TORONTO • NEW YORK • LONDON
AMSTERDAM • PARIS • SYDNEY • HAMBURG
STOCKHOLM • ATHENS • TOKYO • MILAN

Published January 1985

This edition published June 1985
ISBN 0 373 25144 0

Printed in Australia by
Griffin Press Limited, Netley, South Australia 5037

PROLOGUE

"Remind me never to drown in your presence." Karl surfaced, sputtering water with his words.

Christa laughed so hard she could barely stay afloat. "I swear," she said, "that's what they taught us in school. Of course, we were in gym class and not in a real lake."

"That would make a difference." Karl's voice was caustic. He paddled alongside her, his hair dark from being wet, his eyes defiantly blue against the golden tan of his face. She moved uncomfortably under his stare, feeling the length of her red hair heavy on her shoulders. *How unfair*, she thought to herself, *that he should tan to that glorious color while I erupt in brown spots.* She could feel the freckles springing out across the bridge of her nose in the warmth of the sun. Then Karl's arrogant mouth parted in a quick smile and he lunged through the water at her.

Christa screamed and dived away from him, but he caught her. "This is the way you save someone who's drowning," he said, looping his arm under her chin, sliding his body beneath hers. "Just relax." She let her body go limp, her head resting on his arm. She could feel the surge of water against her as his legs propelled them toward the shore of the little pond. The water was warm near the surface where she floated. Above them the sun hung low in the sky, weighted down with heat excessive for June. Christa was conscious of Karl's arm around her neck, the pull and release of his muscles, his finely molded profile just inches from her face.

They reached the shallows and Karl stood up, keeping his hold on her so that she was in front of him, close against his body, her toes digging into the soft pond mud. Her heart started its traitorous tattoo. These past few weeks she had not been able to get within two feet of him without her heart carrying on like this.

"That, my girl, is how it's done." He whispered the words, his lips against her ear. It was too much. Something close to pain knifed through her and her legs went weak with the force of it.

"Christa!" His bantering turned to concern. "Are you all right?" He peered anxiously into her face.

For a brief moment a voice inside her said, *Hide it, close your eyes, look away, don't let him see!* But she was tired of hiding behind the facade of a childish, high school girl, while he pretended a big-brother friendship. So she left her emotions where they were, shining out of her eyes where he would have to recognize and deal with them.

She saw his expression falter, his eyes deepen, and still she refused to mask anything.

"Christa?" The word was a soft question. "Dear God, Christa." He wound his arms around her tight as a steel band, and she stood on her toes, her arms

Can you feel the electricity between us?"

Karl's voice was husky, and his breath came faster as his hands roamed her body.

Christa gasped, feeling the tingles his touch sent through her. "I can...I can feel it."

Karl stroked her softly, then slid down the fleecy pants of her workout suit. "How beautiful you are," he whispered reverently.

Christa's heart pounded as he peeled the rest of her clothing away. Then he stood over her, his lean body tense with excitement, and his gaze promised her everything she'd dreamed of....

THE AUTHOR

The two areas of Ethel Paquin's life that have brought her the most satisfaction are motherhood and writing. A resident of Ridgefield, Connecticut, Ethel and her husband—her high-school sweetheart—have devoted themselves to raising "three wonderful children, a neurotic dog, an even more neurotic horse and two ducks."

"Motherhood's behind me now," says Ethel, "and writing's stretched before me. Right now life looks mighty good!" *Summer Wine* is her first Harlequin Temptation.

clasping him to her. His tongue parted her lips, probing her mouth. His hand traced the line of her shoulder, then impatiently pushed away the top of her bathing suit to cup her breast. She moaned, and he pulled her down on the lush spring grass. Licking the moisture from her breast, he circled her nipple, his tongue massaging it to firmness.

"Karl, Karl." She tangled her fingers in his wet hair, pressing him closer to her. A fire burned in her, frightening and exhilarating. He kissed her eyes, her cheeks, her lips, as if the taste of her skin drove him mad. His hands possessed her, dipping beneath the scant protection of her bikini bottom, making her skin flame.

There was no thought in her mind of stopping him, that her parents might find them, out behind the house, or that they might be doing something wrong. On the contrary, she thought what they were doing was supremely right. She had been longing for this moment, dreaming of it for months, balancing on a narrow ledge of fear that Karl would go back to Germany before it had a chance to happen.

Christa clung to him. This time she was truly drowning, overwhelmed by a sea of emotion and feeling. She knew instinctively that Karl could save her, could release her from the tension surging inside her. "Please," she begged him, "please."

He was as possessed as she was, and covering her body with his, parted her legs with his urgency. She was fleetingly shocked by a sense of invasion when he entered her, but as he moved against her and she felt the heat of their lovemaking building in both of them, she was lost to all rational thought.

She arched against his slim, straining body, holding on, willing to go wherever it was he was taking them. A tidal wave engulfed them, lifting them beyond anyone's reach, carrying them light-years away, leaving them finally limp and exhausted in a place that, for Christa at least, was an undiscovered planet in a universe of unimaginable beauty.

She opened her eyes slowly, almost afraid to see this new world, this strange and foreign place where love had deposited her. What she saw she would always remember. Karl's face hung above hers, his sensitive mouth parted and still soft with passion, his cheeks flushed with fulfillment. But as she watched, his eyes, the brilliant blue of a perfect sky, darkened and she saw something in them that frightened her.

"What have I done?" he whispered.

"Something wonderful." She sighed luxuriously.

Christa traced the worried line of his brows and placed her palm against the sharp plane of his cheek. "Listen to me, Karl von Klee. I'm tired of waiting for you, tired of being treated like a child. I'm old enough to know my own mind. Please don't shut me out. I'll grow up fast, I promise."

He kissed her gently, as if they had all the time in the world that summer, when she was eighteen and he was twenty-five.

They were lovers through the lazy days of June and the torpid nights of July and the heavy, humid afternoons of August. But when the first clear, bright mornings of September dawned, Karl had gone, and in an attempt at self-preservation, Christa hid from her conscious awareness how much of her had gone with him.

1

MEN ARE not a constantly renewable resource, though that would have been hard to prove by the way Christa Monroe disposed of them.

"Good night, Brian. Good night, good night, good night." The words followed a firm push at the small of the man's back, sending him reluctantly into the hallway of Christa's Boston brownstone.

Still shrugging into his jacket halfway down the stairs, her rebuffed suitor called, "You know, Christa, you're a little too old for the vestal virgin bit." Then he turned, to brush angrily against Elizabeth Stefanelli, who was making her way past him to her apartment one floor below Christa's. Elizabeth looked up at her friend standing at the head of the second-story landing, and they waited while Brian's steps pounded down the remaining stairs and the front door banged shut.

"What was the matter with that one?" Elizabeth asked.

"His socks were purple," Christa said, and dashed back into her apartment. Once inside she had to laugh. Some men got so upset at the simple word, "no." And vestal virgin, while inappropriate, was at least an original insult.

She straightened the kitchen, moving her mother's week-old letter from one side of the narrow counter to the other. While she had it in her hand she considered throwing it away, as she had at least once a day since it had come. She ended up sticking it behind the sugar bowl. Then, giving the table a final swipe, she tossed the dishcloth into the sink, picked up her book and settled into one corner of her new living-room couch. Absently she stroked the navy-blue geometric print, admiring again how well it went with the deep red Oriental rug and pale blue wing chair. The apartment was really coming together, except for the limp lace curtains at the window. They were the next project. The drapes she wanted were expensive. They would cost, in Elizabeth's words, a small fortune. Christa was saving her money to buy them. It would take a while, but they were worth waiting for. The right things always were, and it pleased her to have everything just the way she wanted it—under control, with no discordant notes.

The clock on the mantel above her nonworking fireplace struck a subdued nine o'clock. She picked up her book, flipped it open to the marker and settled in for another quiet Friday evening.

On Saturday, Christa cleaned the apartment and did her washing and by four o'clock was done for the day. Sitting with her stocking-clad feet resting on the polished surface of the butler's-tray coffee table, she shivered. Earlier in the day she had opened the windows, because Boston, true to form, had fooled her into thinking it was spring. Now it felt as if winter was putting on a repeat performance, and the wool slacks and bright green Shetland sweater she had on weren't as comfortable as they had been one short hour ago.

She walked to the window and closed it, pausing to look out on the narrow twisting street full of old brownstone houses just like the one she lived in. She was two short blocks off Beacon Hill, and though the neighborhood was a little down-at-the-heel, some of the charm of Beacon spilled over onto Claiborne Street, at considerably more affordable rents than those of the homes above her on the hill.

She was thinking about the letter again. If she kept this up she'd go stark raving mad.

She did a military about-face, walked to the kitchen, crumpled the letter and dropped it into the wastebasket, then just as promptly fished it out again. She opened the envelope and spread the one sheet of writing paper on the counter, smoothing out the wrinkles. It was full of gossipy news from home.

Her father, on his spring teaching break, had persuaded her mother to plant flowers on the far bank of the pond, something he'd been trying to persuade her to do for years. Maria Garcia, once Christa's babysitter, was getting married. Christa had always loved Maria's name and as a child had skipped around the house chanting it like a song. If Maria, who was thirty-four, eight years older than Christa, could finally find someone to settle down with there was certainly hope for Christa, or so her mother rather pointedly hinted. Grandma O'Brien had a new beau—and this one earned more social security than

Grandma did and was able to beat her at poker. The family definitely thought of him as a suitable match. Then near the end of the letter Christa's mother had written, almost as an afterthought: "Karl was here. He drove up from Boston for the day. He's just as gallant as ever, though things in Germany are not going well at the moment. The winery's in trouble. It seems to me it was always in trouble, but this time I gather things are somehow worse than usual. He's here to try and increase sales. Dad was awfully glad to see him; it's been three years. He asked about you and we told him you had started your own business and were doing very well. You'll have to excuse us, we do tend to brag. Daddy told him about your successes with Caldwell, Limited, and he was very impressed. He said something about wanting to talk to you about that. Caldwell's problems seem to be similar to problems at the winery. Why don't you call him? He asks about you every time he comes; you two always got on so well. He's at the St. Pierre."

Christa let her eyes drift from the letter to the small round mirror on the wall beside her. Her earnest face stared back—small featured with shadowy gold-green eyes, skin lightly freckled without the camouflage of makeup, surrounded by a heavy fall of auburn hair. "Karl von Klee wants to talk about business." The words hung softly in the air above her head. She ran her hands over her body, full breasted, round hipped, lithe and attractive; gone was the adolescent eighteen-year-old she'd been the last time she'd seen him.

"And what does your present physical condition have to do with anything? If you expect he'll take one look at you and regret what he's been missing the past eight years, you're more of a fool than I thought. Karl von Klee and his winery can go bankrupt." She said the last words clearly, pausing between each one for emphasis. "I couldn't care less what happens to him."

This time she dropped the letter into the garbage and ran the whole mess downstairs before she could change her mind again. Some kids were playing ball in the street, a sure sign of spring. The sun hung like a giant searchlight at the foot of the hill and stretched her shadow long behind her. She dropped the bag in the trash can and hurried back into the house. On impulse she knocked on Elizabeth's door. "Just thought I'd say hello. Is Mark here?"

"Nope, come on in." Elizabeth held the door open. "How come you never want to come in if he's here? Don't you like him?"

"I like him fine, I just don't want to interrupt anything. Besides, he keeps trying to fix me up with his friends."

"He knows better than that. He's seen the walking wounded." Elizabeth's smile was wicked.

"Thanks," Christa said, tossing a pillow at her friend.

"Your time will come, be patient," teased Elizabeth.

"Or maybe I should break something and be *a* patient."

"That was my ploy, love. You'll have to find your own."

One morning Elizabeth had changed her entire life by the simple decision to walk to work instead of taking the bus. She had tripped on a faulty bit of sidewalk and broken her leg. As a result, she had ended up in the hospital, missed an important meeting and lost a promotion. And while she was lying on her bed of pain grieving over her phenomenally bad luck, Dr. Mark Durham had comforted her, then dated her, then asked her to marry him. Now she sported a lovely emerald-cut diamond and smiled at the drop of a hat.

Looking totally content, Elizabeth settled herself on a couch of the same general age and description as the chair where Christa sat. Both pieces had seen better days.

"So what wonderful thing are you doing tonight?" Christa asked, thinking dismally that her voice had a whine to it.

"Tonight we are eating at La Stella and then going to a movie. Then Mark has . . . ."

"Forget it, I don't want to hear the rest."

Elizabeth's soft, brown eyes clouded, "Are you upset with me?"

"Of course not, I'm envious! Disgustingly, avariciously envious."

"You are not," Elizabeth said, her sunny smile back. "You wouldn't date Mark and you know it. Don't deny it—it doesn't bother me. I think Mark is wonderful but I know you wouldn't give him a second look. I swear, Christa, sometimes I think you're looking for perfection—and perfection doesn't exist, in men *or* women." She leaned forward to impart this last bit of wisdom and now she stood up. "Want some wine? Or would you prefer coffee?"

Christa trailed after her into the kitchen, a trifle annoyed by Elizabeth's smugness. She was not holding out for perfection. She was just not willing to settle for anything less than what she wanted. Once, a long time ago, someone had fulfilled all her desires. Until that happened again—and each year it seemed less likely—she'd remain unattached.

"What's on *your* agenda tonight?" Elizabeth asked over her shoulder as she reached for the jar of coffee.

"Tonight?" Christa played with the teaspoon Elizabeth had set in front of her on the yellow plastic tablecloth. "Ah yes, tonight." Christa was sure she had admitted to Elizabeth, either before or after the event, that she had spent the past four weekends soaking in a hot tub reading mysteries. Something in her rebelled against doing it again. "I'm thinking of calling an old friend," she said, and although it was a lie, her stomach contracted at the thought.

"Oh?" Elizabeth turned to look at her, hooking her short black hair behind her ears. "Anyone I know?"

"No, he goes back before I met you—back to high school, as a matter of fact." She moved her hands to let Elizabeth place a mug of coffee on the table. "He's German. He stayed with us for a couple of years while he was going to school."

"Exchange student?"

"Sort of."

"What do you mean, sort of?"

Christa shrugged. "It was a little more complicated than that." She was lost in thought for a moment, tangled again in sticky memories.

"That could be exciting," Elizabeth ventured, looking at her with a curious expression.

"He's probably bald and fat by now." And wouldn't that be something? If, after all these years, Karl von Klee had no more appeal for her than did Mark Durham. As if in answer to her thoughts, the door bell rang and Elizabeth went to answer it, coming back to the kitchen with Mark. She busied herself getting another cup of coffee and Mark stood in the doorway rocking on his heels. Christa knew he would put his hands in his pockets in a minute and jingle his change. Sometimes, if his pockets were full, he made so much noise it was hard to carry on a conversation.

"How's it going, Christa?" he greeted, his hands moving toward their rendezvous with destiny.

"Not bad." She smiled at the slightly overweight, benevolent-looking man Elizabeth had promised to marry. *She's right*, she thought, *I couldn't have done it*. The idea of going to bed with Mark seemed ludicrous.

"Don't go on my account," he said as she started to rise, his voice barely audible over the jingle of coins.

"I just dropped in for a minute; I've got things to do. I'll let myself out," she said to Elizabeth, who was standing uncertainly by the stove, an empty cup in her hand. "See you soon."

She opened the door to her apartment and headed for the refrigerator. But as she passed the telephone hanging silently on the wall, she stopped and looked at it. She could move the dial in a certain, prescribed way and like magic the past would be alive for her once more. *The past is only a prologue to the future.* Someone had said that once, probably her grandmother. And mistakes are supposed to teach you something. Her grandmother had said that, too.

If only it were as simple as her mother thought, as Christa had pretended to Elizabeth. If she and Karl had simply been good friends who "always got on so well" with each other. She closed her eyes tightly, shaken by a sudden, aching need to see him. It had happened before. Walking down Commonwealth Avenue she would see a tall, slender man with hair of a certain blond shade and for a few blocks Christa would be eighteen again.

What would they talk about if she were actually dumb enough to call him? "I can't keep thinking about this anymore." She spoke the words aloud. "Dial the number, see him—or better yet, let him see you. Let him see what you've been able to accomplish with your life. Then maybe you can forget him."

Her hands shook as she dialed the number. "Is this Karl von Klee?" she said when the deep voice answered. There was a throbbing moment of silence, and Christa's legs gave under her. She slid down along the kitchen wall until she was sitting on the floor. "Never in a million years will you guess who this is." The silence went on for a beat more, while her heart virtually stopped. "You were probably the best cyclist I've ever met."

"My God," the vibrant voice said, the words holding just the trace of an accent, "is that you, Christa?"

Afterward, when she had hung up, two things struck her. The first was that if fate hadn't wanted her to see him, he would have been out. She'd never have called him twice. The second was that he'd recognized her voice almost as quickly as she had recognized his.

They had agreed to meet at the St. Pierre, and Christa went through most of what hung in her closet trying to decide what to wear. Her bedroom was a mess, clothes strewed over everything. She stood in front of her mirror in a lime-green wool dress, its long sleeves ending in narrow ruffles edged in bright blue braid. There was an identical ruffle at the throat. The bodice was unadorned, skimming her slim torso, then belling out in a gentle fullness beneath her waist. Karl had always insisted that green was her color. It came to her with a shock how much of her wardrobe was still that bright shade, even her old ratty bathrobe.

"Karl, Karl," she said softly, "what a legacy you left me." She checked her makeup one more time. There was no sense in trying to put it all on again; her hands were no steadier now than they had been twenty minutes ago. If anything, they were worse.

There was no sense in any of this. She should call the hotel and tell him she wasn't coming. But she didn't, and stepping over a plaid skirt, she put on her coat and left the apartment.

Christa threaded her cranky Datsun through the tangle of Sunday evening traffic, the taillights ahead of her moving like a lava flow. Cars in the city were little more than a nuisance except on rare occasions like tonight when they were indispensable. She braked sharply in front of the St. Pierre and swerved into a parking place. A stinging screech of brakes behind her made her screw up her face, waiting for the clang of metal that never came. The other car swung past and its driver gave her a disgusted look and shook his head.

She sat for a moment watching the people going in and out of the lobby. They looked as if they knew what they were doing, which put them one step ahead of her. This was definitely a mistake. "Please let him be faded and seedy-looking," she prayed as she got out of the car.

The St. Pierre was a hotel in the grand old sense of the word—no chrome, or glass, or sharply angled plastic pieces. It was all good solid wood, heavy upholstery, lush carpet and striated marble. Christa left her name with the desk clerk and walked to one of the velvet-draped windows to look out at the street and wait. Her heart was banging away in her chest so loudly she was sure the woman sitting to her left, idly riffling the pages of *Up-Country Living*, could hear it. She placed her hand over it and willed it to be still.

The carpet silenced his approach so that when he

said, "Christa?" she jumped and whirled to face him, visibly unsettling the woman with the magazine. He was smiling at Christa, his thin, patrician face creased with pleasure. His eyes above a finely molded nose blazed out at her, brilliantly blue beneath the heavy line of his brows. There was a scar on the left side of his jaw above a chin that was squared as if by a draftsman's precise measurements. His thatch of blond hair was still parted on the side and worn in a shaggy cut. She knew it was too heavy to be worn any other way. He had told her that one day when she'd tangled her fingers in it and commented on its thickness. *What a thing to remember now.* She was blushing.

Karl walked purposefully toward her with that agile grace that was so indefinably his. The jacket of his dark gray suit was unbuttoned and the silk of his shirt gleamed in the lamplight. He was as slender as he'd ever been, with not an ounce of excess flesh apparent anywhere. But that slim build belied well-developed muscles and a surprising strength. Christa's breathing apparatus had stopped working and she had to force air into her lungs. This evening showed every promise of becoming a total fiasco. Taking two hesitant steps forward to meet him, she held a smile steady on her face with every ounce of energy she could muster. Karl took her cold, shaking fingers into hands whose touch she had never quite forgotten.

"I can't believe you're here," he said in the seductive voice that made her think of whipped cream. His eyes slid over the gentle swell of her breasts. "You haven't changed a bit."

"No?" She managed to get the word out past the storm that was going on inside her.

Karl's gaze held hers and the tension was almost visible. Then his smile broadened and he was laughing. He pulled her to him and hugged her, the familiar scent of his after-shave dizzying her. "It's very, very good to see you." His arm slipped around her shoulders and he propelled her toward the dining room. "Let's go eat—we have years to catch up on."

Their meeting seemed very easy for Karl, with no gray shades from the past to cloud it. Christa remembered her bedroom, knee-deep in discarded clothing. She thought of the agonizing hours she had spent deciding whether or not to call him. Suddenly, she had an almost uncontrollable urge to bring the point of her heel down sharply on the soft leather toe of his shoe.

They were seated at a small table in one corner of the ornate room. The walls were paneled in dark wood, and the ceiling was crossed with heavy beams. An immense crystal chandelier hung in the center directly over a round table with a surface of inlaid wood. A large basket of fresh flowers had been placed under the chandelier.

Karl started to say something to the waiter hovering at his elbow, then he turned to Christa. "I was about to order for you, but I have no idea what you'd like. I assume you've graduated from Shirley Temples?"

"Some time ago," she assured him. She searched in her mind for something to order. She had never learned to drink hard liquor and she had never developed a taste for wine. What she really wanted was a root beer, but for obvious reasons she wasn't going to order one. "I'll have a Kir," she told the waiter, dragging the word out of her past.

Karl raised his eyebrows. "What do you know about Kir?"

"Boston is a cosmopolitan city, Karl—good things get around."

"Two Kirs," he told the waiter, then turned back to her. "I'm impressed."

"Because I've had Kir? Someone I was dating last year introduced it to me. I had some in his apartment," Christa said, amused at the emotions that flickered through Karl's eyes.

"Ah, yes." There was an odd expression in his voice. "His apartment. I guess your Shirley Temple days are truly over."

You should know. The thought was piercing. *You helped chase them.* "What are you looking at?" she asked as his eyes searched her face.

"You've turned out to be very beautiful."

"And that surprises you?"

"Not really. I always thought you were beautiful." His smile faltered just a little and Christa realized he was less at ease than he had at first appeared. The thought was disquieting. It meant that he felt it too—whatever it was hovering in the air between them.

"So," he said, avoiding her eyes. "Tell me everything."

Everything. The word splashed her with pain.

There wasn't a lot; there could have been so much more. "Well—" she steadied herself with a breath "—I went to college, but you know that." At graduation there had been a bouquet of roses for her and a card that said simply, "Karl." "After school I worked for a short time at Valarian here in Boston, but I didn't get along with the management."

How innocent she had been then—right out of college, sporting a degree in business like a carnation in her buttonhole and holding the knowledge that she had graduated magna cum laude like a shield against failure. Neither the carnation nor the shield had protected her at Valarian, alas. What happened was something that none of her professors at Boston University had seen fit to teach her.

"What was the problem—philosophical differences?"

"No, it was hands. Mr. Valarian's. It's not an unusual problem," she said in answer to the look on his face.

"I suppose not."

"Then I worked with Merkle and Richards. It's a marketing firm in Cambridge."

"Were the men better behaved there?"

"I didn't work with men. I supervised a small department of women. But the men I did come in contact with there were very circumspect. There were two of them, they were both in their seventies, and they owned the firm."

"And now?"

"Now I'm in business for myself as a consultant, helping small businesses create a public image."

"Do you like it?"

"Very much," she said, smiling brightly and holding the smile just a beat too long. "It takes up almost all my time, but it's very gratifying. Of course, I'm just starting out, so my list of clients isn't impressive—yet."

"No matter how small your client list may be, you single-handedly increased one of your clients' profits twice over."

"Caldwell, Limited," she acknowledged with a smile. "It's nice to have a press agent."

The waiter set down two crystal wineglasses filled with rich amethyst liquid. Karl picked his up and extended it toward her. She raised hers and the glasses touched with a sharp little ring.

"To a wonderful evening," Karl declared.

"I'll drink to that." Christa smiled and sipped the sweet, fruity drink.

"Continue," Karl said after he had sampled his own.

"There's not much more to tell."

"I can't believe that."

Christa searched her mind for something that he might find interesting. College exploits? Those days were so far behind her that even she wasn't interested in them anymore. Her meteoric climb in the business world? Aerobic dancing, for Pete's sake? *What*, she asked herself in dismay, *have I done with the past eight years of my life?*

Karl studied her intently. "Are there no men lurking about?"

She tipped her wineglass so that the contents

swirled dangerously close to the rim. What an impossible question to answer. She decided to play it light. "Of course, my father comes by all the time, and Grandma O'Brien is always trailing some new beau into Boston to meet me."

He sat back in his chair and laughed out loud. "That outrageous woman! What's she up to these days? Still playing poker?"

Christa nodded, grinning.

The humor in his face subsided slowly and they sat silently facing each other. Christa saw his eyes darken, the expression in them alter subtly, and it was all there between them again, as if the intervening years had never been. She lowered her lids against the intensity of her feelings.

"You haven't answered my question," he said.

"Yes, I have." She chose not to hide behind any more games.

He toyed with his own glass, moving it so that the liquid whirled around inside in a miniature whirlpool. "I'd heard you were engaged." He studied his drink as if the answer were going to come from it rather than her.

He must mean Paul. Sweet, warm, loving Paul, who had trailed after her through the last two years of college, doing so much for her with so little in the way of payment it had been embarrassing. It hadn't seemed to matter how many times she'd told him she didn't love him—the words never made it beyond his ears. She remembered his face the last time she'd seen him, when she'd said goodbye. She'd wanted to tell him she wasn't worth all that sadness, but she doubted he'd believe her. What a responsibility someone else's happiness was.

"No, I was never engaged. I was seeing someone and my mother wished it into an engagement, but it never really was."

"It's hard to believe that someone like you doesn't have a dozen men waiting in line for your attentions."

"I never was one to play the field." She would not, or could not, play games. Once she had decided a relationship was going nowhere, she refused to see the man again. One by one they stopped calling, except for a few who had successfully made the change from pursuer to friend.

Karl was partly to blame for that. Over the years, whenever a relationship collapsed under its own sodden weight or vaporized because of its lack of substance, some niggling bit of Christa's consciousness was aware that the man had been compared to Karl and found wanting. What was it that had flamed so brightly between them that it had permanently impaired her vision?

"What are you thinking about so deeply?"

There was a sudden little surge of anger in Christa. "What about you?" she asked. Let *him* be on the defensive for a while. "Who are the women in your life?"

"We don't have time to talk about all of them." He tried joking but wasn't quite able to carry it off. He made careful intersecting circles with the bottom of his wineglass. "I'm afraid I, too, must admit that there is no one of any importance in my life."

"How sad," she said softly before she could stop herself. There had been a hint of something in what Karl had said. Maybe he had ended up as much a cripple from their affair as she had.

He was saved from answering her by the appearance of an immense leather-bound menu and a waiter who stood discreetly by to answer any questions Christa might have regarding the food.

"We'll have the Kabinett with the appetizer and the Spätlese with dinner," Karl said.

"Von Klee wines?"

"Unless you'd prefer something else?"

"No." She studied the entrées, but her stomach rebelled at the thought of food. She finally ordered the first thing on the menu—baked stuffed crab with asparagus, and marinated artichoke hearts for an appetizer. Karl was watching her across the flickering light of two low, pink candles. Christa could see the tiny flames reflected in the bottomless blue of his eyes. Another flame flickered deep inside her, licking at her nerve endings. Their eyes held a fraction of a second too long for her to simply look away as if nothing had happened. She searched desperately in a mind that had turned to mud for something to say to break the silence, but it was Karl who spoke. "Tell me about Caldwell. Your father said they deal in imported fabrics."

"Woolens, mostly from Scotland."

"Tartans, tweeds?"

"And other things too. They bring in woolens now that are as delicate as silk, and twice as expensive." How wasteful to be talking about fabric when what she really wanted to know was, did he remember the feel of her body as clearly as she remembered his?

"Is your dress Scottish wool?"

She pulled herself back to the conversation. "Yes, but not the kind I was just talking about. But this has a fairly nice hand." She smoothed the fabric over her knees.

"A nice hand?" Karl asked, puzzled.

"That's a word used to describe the weight and feel of wool and how it drapes. This isn't bad." She stretched her arm across the table so that he could touch the fabric. He ran his fingers gently down the green wool and left a throbbing line from her elbow to her wrist. She was completely flustered. He had always been able to do that to her. There had never been any shield she could erect to protect herself from Karl, and apparently there still wasn't.

"I'd love the chance to get back to Scotland again and see the fabric made. A lot of it comes from small individual family businesses. They raise their own sheep, card the wool, spin it and weave it themselves." Christa was talking too fast, but she couldn't seem to stop. "Often we get twenty or thirty yards of material that has no equal anywhere in the world."

To her profound relief the waiter arrived with the appetizers before Christa had a chance to run the subject of wool completely into the ground. He uncorked the bottle, waiting while Karl sniffed the cork and then sipped the wine itself. Karl nodded and the waiter filled both glasses.

"Should we toast again? To us," he said simply and touched her glass with his.

Christa raised a surprisingly steady hand to her mouth and tasted the crisp, dry liquid.

"Do you like it?" Karl asked.

She hesitated. "I'm not an expert on wines. To be honest with you, I don't much like them."

"That's blasphemy!" His expression was so incredulous that for the first time in this long, tense evening she laughed, a deep spontaneous laugh. Then, because she was so nervous, she found it hard to stop.

"You can't be so uneducated as to really mean that. Stop laughing, this is serious." A small smile lurked around his mouth.

"I know it." She struggled to keep her face solemn.

"Taste it again," he ordered.

She did, this time paying attention to what she was drinking. "You're right—this is really very good."

"That's better." Erik watched to see if she had only said that to appease him, but when she sipped more with obvious pleasure, he relaxed.

Christa was able to keep up a light, pleasant conversation over dinner. She was even able to eat, which was a good thing; it would have been criminal to waste the perfectly prepared meal. Then the evening was over, and Erik was walking her to her car.

"I've enjoyed tonight very much," he said. "Why haven't we done this before?"

"I can't imagine," she said dryly.

"I guess the past does die hard," he acknowledged. "Has it died?" he asked suddenly. "Have you finally forgiven me."

"Of course," she said quickly, as if he were foolish to ask. "I forgave you a long time ago."

"I'm glad." He held out his hand for her keys and unlocked the car door for her. Then he bent and kissed her lightly on the cheek. "Good night, *Liebchen*. Drive safely."

She barely remembered getting home at all, until she reached her bedroom and was faced with the disorder she had left behind.

2

CHRISTA CHECKED her watch as she ran lightly up the steps to her apartment, holding closed the jacket of her beige wool suit. The wind still blew from the harbor and it was damp and cold. The safety of the vestibule was a relief, and she took a minute to smooth her hair before continuing up the two flights of stairs to her apartment on the top floor. As she rounded the first flight she saw Elizabeth poised with her key in the door, watching the stairway.

"I wondered if that was you," Elizabeth said, completing the turn of the key and opening her door. "Want to come for supper? Mark's on duty tonight."

"I can't tonight," Christa said. "Company's coming."

"Oh?" Elizabeth's eyes followed her up the stairs. "Who?"

"Karl," Christa called back. "He's the exchange student I mentioned."

"Aha!" Elizabeth walked to the foot of the stairs. "Should I begin to worry?"

"Not yet," Christa said, struggling with her own key. "I'll let you know if and when." The door opened and she entered her apartment.

Once inside, she stood dead still, as if a switch had

been turned off. She was unnerved by her behavior—running from the bus stop, taking the
stairs at twice her normal speed. It had been a mistake to tell Karl he could come at six o'clock—six
was too early. But his call yesterday had surprised
her and without thinking she had agreed to the
time. Actually, the mistake had been in telling him
he could come at all. She hadn't thought she would
hear from him. She had coaxed herself into believing it would be for the best, and that, given some
time, she might be able to sort out her feelings and
reach some conclusions about what had really happened in the dining room of the St. Pierre.

With a start she realized precious moments had
slipped by and, hurrying to her bedroom, she
quickly stripped off her suit and shrugged into her
bathrobe. In the kitchen she removed a bowl of
dough from the refrigerator where it had been rising
all day. Holding it in one arm she reached across the
counter for the flour canister, overturning the sugar
bowl in the process.

"Damn it!"

Christa brushed the sugar into a pile and swept it
back into the bowl, pushing it out of the way; then
plopped the dough out onto the counter where it
landed with a satisfying "thwunk." She looked at it
in dismay. She hadn't sprinkled any flour under it.
Raising the dough a bit to see how badly it was
stuck, she found the under side garnished with glittering crystals of sugar.

"Sweet homemade garlic bread—another Monroe
culinary achievement." Her voice was tight with

frustration. Slapping the doughy mound with the flat of her hand, she turned her back on it. She gripped the edge of the counter behind her, barely under control. Even at eighteen she hadn't acted like this. She made herself walk back to the bedroom and sit on the edge of the cherry-wood four-poster that had cost her a month's salary.

"Two deep breaths," she instructed and waited for them to take effect. Her eyes concentrated on the flowered wallpaper, the ruffled organdy curtains, the small oval braided rugs. The room was warm and friendly, a refuge. In the evenings after all her chores were done, she would take a hot bath and nestle under the down quilt with whatever book she was reading until her eyes were heavy with sleep. Sometimes she would wake at two or three in the morning, the book still in her hands, the light still burning.

It used to bother her that she went to bed with a book instead of a man. Several men had commented unkindly about her preference. She had chalked up their unflattering assessment of her to sour grapes. She was not a virgin, but there was nothing about sex simply for its own sake that attracted her. There had to be something more. It was probably love, though she shied from the term. She didn't understand it and, to her knowledge, had not experienced it. She still wasn't sure what it was that she and Karl had once shared.

What was Karl doing right now, she wondered. Was he mooning around, hyperventilating at the thought of seeing her again?

"In a pig's eye," she said.

He was probably putting the finishing touches on his shave, selecting one of his thousand-dollar outfits and going over in his mind what it was he wanted to ask her about Caldwell, Limited. After all, she reminded herself, that was why he had wanted to see her in the first place. Wouldn't he be surprised when he opened her door to find that she had become a puddle of butter and was nothing more than a stain on her kitchen floor? She should never have started this. With a modicum of luck she could arrange it so that he broke her heart again. The telephone rang and she jumped as if it were wired directly to her.

"I need to know what you're planning for dinner," Karl said, "so I can bring something suitable to drink."

Goaded by a diffuse anger that had been an on-and-off companion these past few days, she answered, "Don't bother. I have some red stuff left over from Christmas. We can drink that." She was chagrined at how small a revenge she had been able to muster and how satisfying even that had been.

There was a rush of exasperated breath, and then silence.

"I was kidding," she said, when the silence had gone on too long.

"I'm deliberating on whether or not you're worth saving."

"From what?"

"A life of deprivation. But because I'm very fond of your parents, I'll make the effort. I'll bring the wine, several bottles of it, and I'll begin the all-important job of teaching you to taste."

"How very kind of you."

"It's nothing. Now, what are we having for dinner?"

"Filet mignon," she said, the rebellion gone out of her. "Baked potato with sour cream, fresh broccoli flown in for the occasion from Georgia and—" she glanced at the baleful lump of dough "—some kind of home-baked bread."

"Sounds wonderful," he said. "I'll see you shortly."

CHRISTA WATCHED HIM come walking up the street, his head bent against the omnipresent wind, his tan, military-type raincoat flapping behind him. He moved with energy and grace, taking the front steps easily despite the two small cases he carried. She left the window and buzzed him in, checking her reflection in the pier glass as she passed it. She wore a pair of faded jeans and a fisherman's knit sweater her grandmother had made—a small attempt at controlling the evening. She would be damned if she was going to get all dressed up for him and give him the idea he was anything more to her than an old friend she had taken pity on. She had not been able to carry the casual attitude all the way, however. Cursing herself for a fool, she had carefully, painstakingly applied fresh makeup and a light misting of perfume. She checked her mascara on her way to the door, but it hadn't smudged in the ten minutes it had been on her lashes.

She opened the door just as Karl was about to knock. His face was flushed from the weather and the climb, and his hair was tousled, giving him a vulnerable look that was completely out of keeping with the person she knew him to be. She eyed the two wooden cases he carried. "Were you planning a long stay? If I remember correctly the invitation was only for dinner."

He rose to her bait. "For your information, I had the hotel pack a supper for two. After all, one never knows what will pass for food in the homes of working girls in this barbaric city."

He deposited the boxes in her living room and shrugged out of his raincoat, passing a hand over his rumpled hair. She faced him this time with some semblance of calm, refusing to allow his eyes to penetrate her inner state, or his smile to turn her stomach inside out. He walked slowly around, pausing in front of a bold geometric needlepoint she had just finished, then turned to survey the room.

"You have lovely taste. Did you do that?" He indicated the piece of needlepoint and smiled when she said yes. "I was sure you had."

"I still have a few things to do in the kitchen, and then we can relax."

Karl followed her down the short hallway that connected the front and back of the apartment. With his hands behind him, he peered over her shoulder as she put the finishing touches on the stuffed mushrooms before slipping them in the oven. He examined the two steaks waiting for the kiss of the broiler and dipped a finger in a small glass bowl of chives and sour cream.

"I'd forgotten what you were like in a kitchen," she said with a laugh, pushing his hand away from the sour cream. It was going to be all right. She was going to be able to handle things. They had slipped back past the end of their old relationship and surfaced somewhere in the middle, where feelings had been honest and easy to deal with.

"I have never been able to forget your mother," Karl said. "She made some kind of Chinese chicken dish. I loved to watch her chop the vegetables. She got this look on her face, as if the fate of the world hung on just how evenly she could cut them." He watched Christa silently while she seasoned the steaks, then said, "Some of the best memories I have are of the time I spent with your family. In some ways you were like my sister. I think that's why I felt so badly about what happened."

Christa paused, the pepper mill quiet in her hands, the life raft she had just settled down in punctured by his soft words. "Stop," she said abruptly. "No more about the past, no memories."

He watched her without answering. Disconcerted, she turned to check the mushrooms, which were nowhere near ready. He was not going to drag her into a discussion of those last few weeks. She had told him once he was forgiven, and he would have to accept that. She straightened up from the oven, her face flushed from the heat, to find him still watching her. Her eyes slid from him to the doorway. "What's in those crates you brought?"

"Crates?" He pushed himself reluctantly away from the wall he had been leaning against and walked into the living room. "These are scientifically designed packing cases," he said, bringing them into the kitchen. He lifted one onto the table and unsnapped the small brass catch that held it closed. Inside were four bottles of wine, each held in its individual compartment by a molded wooden bar. "Let's see," he said, studying the four bottles in front of him. "This one, I think." He removed one of the wooden bars and slipped the wine bottle out. "Do you have a corkscrew?"

"Don't you use your teeth? I was sure wine connoisseurs, macho wine connoisseurs, used their teeth." It had always been so easy to tease him.

"If I remember correctly," he said, his voice a silky thread, "your flippant answers used to get you into trouble."

Suddenly, they were back in her mother's kitchen, Karl's hands locked on her wrist, bending her arm behind her back. "Take that back," he had said, his face inches from hers, and then he'd had to kiss her to stop her from laughing. The clarity of the memory shocked her and she fought it down. "The corkscrew is in the drawer next to the sink."

"That's better."

She bent to check the mushrooms again and, hardly looking at them, took them from the oven and slipped them on a plate. After standing for a moment with the empty pan in her hand, trying to regain control of herself, she put the sizzling, sausage-stuffed caps on a tray, refusing to worry about whether the pork was cooked through or not. *If we get food poisoning,* she vowed, *let it be on his conscience.* Adding some glasses and napkins that, much to Karl's disgust, said "Let's Have a Gouda Time," she carried the tray to the living room. Karl followed with the wine and filled their glasses.

"Will you be upset if I don't like it?" Christa asked.

"Upset is not the word. There's a ritual to drinking wine. Hold your glass like this and rotate it, looking at the color." In the twilit room the wine glowed a pale amber. "Now, scent it. Everything about a wine is revealed by its scent. Did you know that your sense of taste is located in your nose?" He raised his glass and inhaled deeply, completely absorbed in what he was doing. Christa followed him and was rewarded by a lovely fragrance.

"You like that?" Karl said, watching her.

"It has a . . . full smell," she said hesitantly, as if unsure that was correct.

"You're right. It has none of the harsh, sharp smell of less perfect wine. Now you can taste it." He raised the glass to his lips and savored some of the liquid before swallowing it.

"I'm not going to do that," she said.

"Do what?"

"Roll it around in my mouth like that."

"It's the only way to get the full flavor."

"Well, I'm not going to do it."

"Don't be ridiculous. Everyone drinks wine like that."

"I don't."

"You don't drink wine."

"My friend Elizabeth does, and she doesn't gargle it."

They sat for a moment looking at each other, Karl's face flushed slightly, and then he laughed softly. "You did it to me again. I'd forgotten how expert you were at it."

"You do tend to get pompous," she said, her lips curving in amusement. Still smiling, she tasted the wine. It flowed into her mouth, light and fruity with just a hint of something else.

"Overtones," Karl explained. "That faint woodsy taste comes from the smoke of house fires. When the grapes are crushed they absorb the smell. The colder the weather, the more fires, the more overtones."

"Do only von Klee wines have them?"

"These particular ones, yes. It has to do with the kinds of things the villagers burn and our location in the valley. The smoke tends to hang in the air and the grapes pick up the taste." He got up from the couch and brought another bottle back from the kitchen. "This one has an entirely different taste. Finish that." He pointed to her half-full glass.

"I thought you weren't supposed to gulp," she complained.

"Gulp, just this once."

They went through the same ritual with the new wine, this time without any objections from Christa. She was delighted to be able to pick up the subtle differences between the two.

"Good," Karl said. "At least you have an educable palate."

She finished the wine in her glass and considered the man who had poured it for her. Here they were, sitting in her living room, with the curtains moving restlessly in the light breeze. The outlines of the furniture were gradually receding as the light faded away through the panes. It was as if Karl had never been away, as if the intervening years had not existed. Things must have been happening all that time, but she couldn't for the life of her remember what any of them had been. Karl sat slouched against the cushions, as lost in thought as she was. Hating to break the mood, she reached toward a table lamp to turn it on.

"Don't do that." Karl stopped her. "I want to say something, and it's better said in the dark. I know we agreed to bury the past, but before I can there's something I need to say. Few things in my life have the power to hurt me as much as the memories of that last summer we spent together." She reached out and put a hand on his arm.

"Let me finish," he said gruffly. "I've wanted to say this to you for years. I behaved in an unprincipled manner. I took the trust your parents gave me and threw it away."

He seemed determined to resurrect the past. As many times as she had forced the memories back to their dark places, he had dragged them out into the light. And now, what she had been fighting against since that dinner at the Pierre overwhelmed her. No amount of self-control could dispel the ghosts . . . or the feelings they brought with them.

"It wasn't all your fault. I was involved, too." Her words barely ruffled the air.

"My sweet girl, you were eighteen. I was twenty-five. I certainly should have been able to stop myself. I need to tell you just once how sorry I am."

Against the dark background of her quiet living room, Christa saw that long-ago summer afternoon—both of them sleek and tan, wet from swimming in the pond behind her parents' house. The pond that this year would be framed in a riot of flowers.

Karl stared at his hands folded tightly in front of him. "Can you really forgive me?"

She fingered her glass, her hand shaking, her voice uncertain. "It was so many years ago. I hated you for a long time, then that passed and gradually I was even able to remember the good times."

He touched her head, smoothing the heavy fall of her hair, lifting the strands and letting them drift from his fingers. "Golden fire," he said.

How many times had he made that observation, caressing her in just this way?

"Christa, at the Pierre, when you turned to face me...." He left the sentence unfinished.

"I know. It can't have been eight years, it seems like only yesterday," she said, speaking softly of the past. "When you left me, I couldn't believe you wouldn't come back. I waited and waited. I dreamed about you all the time."

"I had no choice, I had to go home. My father had died, my uncles were waiting for me to take over. There was nothing I could do."

"You could have married me." The words were out before she realized she was going to say them.

The bitterness in her voice after all these years amazed her.

"You were a child! You were barely out of high school!" His voice rose angrily. "Is that what you expected?"

"You left me very easily."

"Not so easily," he answered with a sigh.

"It seemed that way to me." She got to her feet. "I'd better start the steaks."

Karl reached for her hand and stopped her. "Don't hate me. In many ways I was a child then, too."

"I don't hate you." She was not altogether sure that was the truth. As she started for the kitchen she felt the anger again, focused this time. Yes, he was asking her forgiveness. But it seemed to her that he was sorry for the wrong thing.

3

NOT BY ANY STRETCH of the imagination could the dinner have been termed relaxing. They talked, they ate, they passed one another the butter and the bread, but the main course of the meal was the well-preserved memory of a summer long past. They avoided acknowledging it, but it was there at the table with them, almost as tangible as the filet and the broccoli.

Karl swallowed the last of his coffee mousse and sighed. "Wonderful. You're an excellent cook."

"There were a few minutes around five o'clock when I'd have bet this meal wouldn't have been worth eating, but it did turn out well after all." Christa reached for the slender, pewter coffeepot she had bought not long ago in a thrift shop. It was an unusual design she had found appealing. It had cost her twelve dollars.

"If it turns out to be aluminum I'm bringing it right back," she had warned the old woman who ran the shop, not believing that anything made of pewter could cost so little. "It's pewter, honey, I guarantee it," the woman told her. "Man who brought it in on consignment just wants to get rid of it." And it had been pewter, appraised at over one hundred dollars. The appraiser had even been able to give her a little background on the piece, since it bore the mark of its maker. He had been a silversmith, then a pewtersmith, then an alcoholic. It had been years since the appraiser had seen any of his work. He hoped the craftsman had gotten back on his feet and was working again. Christa was embarrassed to tell him where she had bought it. Each time she used the coffeepot she said a silent prayer that the man who had made it had pulled himself together. It had become one of her treasured possessions—not because of its monetary value, but for what it was worth in terms of human feelings.

She filled their cups and told the story to Karl.

"Ahh, that hurts," he said. "He must have lost all his self-esteem to have done something like that. When that's gone there's not much left."

"Maybe someone came along and helped him get back on his feet."

"Spoken like a true romantic," he said.

"Don't you believe that can happen?"

"That someone might have come along and helped him get his life back together? Yes, I think that's possible. That it restored his self-esteem? That's another question. Self-esteem by the very meaning of the word is something no one else can give you. You earn it yourself." He studied the steaming black liquid in his cup and Christa knew he was thinking about something personal. "And you lose it yourself."

She scanned his face and he sat quietly under her scrutiny. "How long will you be in Boston?" she finally ventured.

"I don't know. Until I get things straightened out."

"My mother said there was some kind of problem with the winery?"

He raised his coffee to his lips, inhaling the aroma before tasting it. When he caught her watching him, he smiled. "I smell everything first. Yes—I wanted to talk to you about the winery, but up until now my mind has been sidetracked. We have a situation in Einzell similar to the one your father described that you handled for Caldwell. You helped them out of it very nicely. What did you do for them?"

"I showed them how to increase their sales."

"Just like that?"

"There was a little more to it. Let me give you some background. Caldwell isn't a large firm, but they've been in business for twenty-five years and they have a fine reputation. They imported high-grade woolens, exactly the sort of fabric you assumed they dealt with the first time we talked—tartans and tweeds. For a long time they did well, but then profits began to slip. Because the woolens were imported, they cost more than those made in the States, and while an expert would see the difference, most people wouldn't.

"There are always people willing to spend the extra money to buy the very best, but then they want their friends to know that's what they've done. If no one can tell the difference between a plaid skirt made from imported fabric and one made by a local manufacturer, what's the use of paying the extra money?" For the first time since they'd sat down to eat, Christa began to relax. She was on sure footing now.

"When I was called in to look over the problem, I spent a lot of time studying their market. Martin Caldwell, one of the owners, was of the opinion that they should import less-expensive fabrics. But the more I thought about it and the more people I talked to, the more I was sure that wasn't the answer. I thought they should go the other way.

"They got a lot of mail from guilds and artisans asking if Caldwell would be willing to represent them. The family had dismissed the idea as impractical; the prices they would have to charge would be astronomical." She paused for a minute to see if she was boring Karl, but he was concentrating completely on her story.

"That summer my parents went to Ireland and as a birthday present they offered me a round-trip ticket, too. While I was over there, I took a side trip to Scotland to visit one of the guilds whose correspondence had intrigued me. I was very impressed. Their fabric was like nothing I'd ever seen. Literally, it was unique."

Karl reached across the table to the coffeepot and refilled his cup, motioning her to continue.

"When I got back I did the selling job of my life on Ian Caldwell, the more adventurous of the brothers. Somehow I persuaded him to give my idea a try. They contracted with the guild to be their sole market here in the States, and then I initiated an advertising campaign, using a firm I have a lot of confidence in. We placed ads in controlled-circulation magazines, where the annual income of readers is well above average. And having discovered I had a talent for selling, I contacted several designer houses and sold them on the idea of using Caldwell fabrics. One of them was Lass Rollan." This last name was said with pride.

"Even *I* know the name," Karl said. "And that was it?"

"That was it," she said. "It does sound simple when you say it, doesn't it? You should have been there, though, when the big decisions were being made. It was anything but simple. If it hadn't worked, the whole company could have gone down the drain and my own very fledgling consulting firm would have gone with it. When I look back on it I can't believe I was so confident. Caldwell was my first big client and the only reason I got them was they couldn't afford the fees the larger firms were charging. I still can't figure out why they went along with me—I was a nobody, really."

"Because your idea was sound and the concept bold, and Ian recognized it." Karl's forehead was creased in concentration. "Importing cheaper fabric would only have prolonged the agony—it wouldn't have made them successful. Eventually they'd have gone under or become one of thousands of little firms hanging on by the skin of their teeth." She could tell from his tone of voice what he thought of that idea.

"What you did," he continued, "was to present a product so unusual, people were willing to come to you and pay your price. That was ingenious."

"Thank you."

There was open admiration in his eyes. "Do you

know," he said thoughtfully, "we have the possibility of doing the same thing at the winery. Von Klee is one of the few places where some wines are still produced by hand."

She let what he said sink in for a moment and then, realizing what he was implying, asked, "You don't *stomp* on the grapes!"

"A little indelicate, but yes, that's exactly what we do."

"That must raise the costs considerably."

"Not as much as you might think. The manpower to do it is still available in Einzell, and the tradition goes back a long way. The biggest problem is that it's so damned inconvenient. But something happens to the grapes when they are sent through a machine. Something is lost. The wine is less perfect. Maybe one person in a hundred can taste the difference, but to that person the difference is important—rather like Caldwell fabric."

"Are you considering increasing the amount of hand-produced wines?"

"Yes. But then I'd have to increase the market for it."

"Would you consider advertising?"

"*I'd* consider it," he said. "The family has other ideas."

"Such as?"

He waved his hand, dismissing them. "I don't want to get into that now. Who handled the advertising for Caldwell?"

"Lewis and Loman," she said, naming one of the city's well-known firms.

"Is there a chance they would talk to me?"

"I don't see why not. Would you like me to set up an appointment?" she offered.

"I'd appreciate it."

And then there didn't seem to be anything else to say. They endured a few heartbeats of tense silence, and then Karl shifted. "I guess I ought to be going. It's late and you're a working girl." He pushed his chair away from the table and stood up. The awkwardness was back. There was no protocol to fit their particular situation, no chapter in etiquette books titled, "How to Say Good-Night to a Former Lover."

She handed him his coat and stepped back while he put it on, reaching up to straighten the back of his collar. "Thanks," he said, pulling the sleeves of his jacket down. "I'm leaving you some wine." They had progressed as far as the hallway.

"You don't have to do that."

"You need the practice. Tomorrow I'm flying to New York to talk to some importers. When I get back on Friday I'll want a complete report on what you thought of the two varieties I left. Oh—and Christa," he added in a softer tone, "I enjoyed tonight very much." And then his mouth touched hers. It was no casual kiss. His lips were soft and warm, moving deliberately over hers.

This is what it feels like to faint. The thought filled Christa's mind and she held on for dear life.

"Good night, Christa. Sleep well." Karl's words were whispered against her cheek, and then he started down the stairs, pausing with his hand on the banister. "You'll contact Lewis and Loman for me?"

"Yes," she agreed. "I'll call Bob Fairfax in the morning." Christa met Karl's eyes and forced herself to hold hers steady. She listened to him descend the stairs, her body inflamed and pulsing. When the front door closed, she ran to her window, barely able to pick him out of the darkness as he made his way down the street to where he had parked his car. She stayed behind the curtains in case he looked up, but he never did. She watched the street long after it was empty and then walked slowly to the kitchen to clear the table.

THE EARLY-MORNING SMELL of breakfast coffee hung in the hallway. Christa inhaled it while she waited impatiently outside Elizabeth's door. "Hurry up!" She knocked again. "We'll miss the bus."

Elizabeth came out, handing Christa her keys. "Here, lock it," she said, bending to fasten the straps on her shoes. They ran down the stairs and then hurried along the sidewalk, Elizabeth buttoning and adjusting all the way to the bus stop. "You're always so together," she complained to Christa.

"If you don't get a little better organized, I'm going to stop waiting for you. These mad rushes leave me frazzled for the rest of the morning." Christa's voice was sharp.

"Sorry," Elizabeth said, her voice subdued.

"No, I'm sorry," Christa returned. "I'm upset with myself and I'm taking it out on you."

"That's what friends are for," Elizabeth said, her smile back. "I've certainly unloaded on you enough times."

Christa gave her a hug. "You're the most even-tempered person I know."

"And all my life I've longed to be tempestuous." She sighed. "Oh well, you can't have everything." They made it to the bus stop in silence and then Elizabeth confessed, "If I were well-mannered, I'd realize you probably don't want to talk about last night, but my curiosity is killing me. How did the dinner go?"

"All right," Christa said over her shoulder as she boarded the bus. "It was strained. After the initial, 'so what have you been doing?' was over with, there wasn't much to say. We mostly talked business. When you haven't seen someone in a long time—" she paused, slipping into a seat "—you don't have much in common anymore." Which wasn't exactly the case with Karl. The problem was more what they *did* have in common than what they didn't.

"Do you think you'll see him again?"

"I don't know."

"Oh, Christa."

"Oh, Christa what?" She sounded a warning.

"All right, I won't say a thing," and as if to emphasize her words, Elizabeth folded her hands and looked resolutely out the window.

Christa knew what she was going to say anyway. *You don't give anyone a chance. You cut them off. What can you tell from one date?* And the corker—

you're not getting any younger. Well, one thing Christa was sure of was that she would not marry simply to escape being unmarried. She wondered if that was what Elizabeth was doing, then dismissed the thought as unfair. Just because Mark Durham did absolutely nothing for her, didn't mean that Elizabeth couldn't be in love with him. That was the thing about love that drove Christa insane. There had been nice, kind, intelligent, good-looking men willing to court her through the years and she had turned her back on all of them. They were too predictable, she said, for want of a better word. That couldn't be said of Karl, for predictable he wasn't! Nor had he proved to be particularly sensitive, thoughtful or kind—all the things Christa would have sworn were at the top of her ten-most-important-traits-in-a-man list. Why, then, had he possessed her physically and emotionally the way no other man ever had? There was some need in her that he alone was able to fill. Their feelings for each other were so tangled, it seemed entirely possible that they would strangle both of them, or suffocate them under the sheer weight of what hung over them unsaid. Obviously it would be better for everyone concerned if she never saw Karl again. Nothing, absolutely nothing, could be gained by starting things up again. She would make the appointment with Bob Fairfax, and that would be that. Karl would go back to Germany and she would go on with her life. It was good she had called him and they had gotten together, she told herself. Maybe now his memory would be less intense for her. This whole episode was definitely a step toward maturity, a putting to rest of old ghosts, and that's how she would look at it. She'd told herself this over and over again last night after he'd left, as she lay in bed, listening to the mantel clock strike eleven and then twelve, with sleep still far away.

"It'll be cheap." Elizabeth's voice sliced through Christa's thoughts. The bus had stopped and Elizabeth was getting off. "Tonight," she repeated, "we're eating Chinese, want to come?"

Christa shook her head. "Thanks, but I've got too much to do. Besides, I'm not in a very good mood."

"Really?" Elizabeth said dryly, "I hadn't noticed. See you tomorrow then."

By TEN O'CLOCK Christa had begun to think she might as well go home, for all the work she was getting done. She was relieved when Katie Warren, her part-time receptionist, opened the door to Christa's office and interrupted her. "Bob Fairfax is here," she said, and stepped back to let him in.

"Office" was a pretentious word to describe the area in which Christa conducted business. It was a small square room with barely enough space for her desk, two chairs and a filing cabinet. But it boasted a narrow view of the Charles River from its one window and it had a good address that served her well on her stationery. At the moment, it was all she could afford, even with the loan her grandmother had given her to get started.

"It's a good investment," Grandma O'Brien had

said. "It's my poker winnings from the past five years. I'll feel less guilty about them if I know they're helping you."

Christa had done what she could to make the room attractive. The walls were white and hung with pieces of her needlepoint and an Andrew Wyeth print. The rug was a deep and satisfying brown, and the tall, old-fashioned window was curtained in sheer white and draped in a tieback of brown, black and white plaid.

Bob Fairfax's stocky frame hinted at restrained energy. As with so many men of his build people were never quite sure if the bulk was muscle or something less solid. "Have you got a minute, Christa? I wanted to show you these." He spread a series of preliminary sketches on her desk. "And I'd like to go over that list of magazines one more time."

She looked over the mock-ups, pointed out two that she really liked and okayed the final list of magazines for Caldwell's winter ads.

"Thank you, ma'am," he said, slipping the ad boards back into his portfolio. "I'll leave you to your work."

"What work?" Christa said. "My mind refuses to concentrate. If you have a minute I'd like to talk."

"Shoot."

"Are you in the market for a new client?"

He stopped what he was doing and looked at her. "My wife is at this very moment negotiating with a travel agency to whisk us from here to the Bahamas and you want to know if I'm in the market for a new client?" He sat down, crossed his legs and leaned back in the chair. "I'm all ears."

"I have a friend who heads an old and very respected winery. His name is von Klee."

"Never heard of him."

"That sums up his problem. The winery is located in Einzell, Germany, and they're interested in increasing their market here in the States. At least that's what I think they want to do. It's a family-owned operation that goes back nine hundred years."

Bob whistled. "That's what I call corporate stability."

"It's amazing, isn't it?" She dropped the crisp, businesslike approach she had assumed in order to make talking about Karl easier. "Karl says the first vines on their hillside were planted by the Romans. Anyway, there's something very special about the white wine they make. It has something to do with chimney smoke and the way the grapes are processed." She broke off to tell him that they still produced some of the wine by hand.

"Come on," he said.

"It gets more unreal. The whole operation is run by the family from a castle that was built in the Dark Ages...." She stopped because Bob had his eyes closed and was shaking his head. "What's the matter?"

"Is his real name Rumpelstiltskin?"

"I know, it sounds crazy but it's true. To hear him talk you'd think the winery had a life of its own." She wondered if Karl had ever gotten that same light in his eyes talking about her as he had telling her about von Klee wines. "Are you interested?"

"Sure, I'll talk to him."

"It may not lead to anything."

"That's life," he said, spreading his hands. "*But* if it does by chance become the biggest money-maker of my short but startling career, you can come to the Islands with us."

"Thanks," Christa said.

"No problem, we were thinking about bringing a baby-sitter anyway."

"You may find this hard to believe," she said wistfully, "but that's the best proposition I've had in quite a while."

CHRISTA WASHED HER SUPPER DISHES, dried them and put them away, hanging the dish towel on its small brass hook. The empty rooms that sometimes seemed restful and on occasion seemed lonely, tonight seemed electrically charged. She moved restlessly from one place to another and finally went into the bathroom, turning on the hot water and scooping two large handfuls of bubble bath into the tub. Maybe a hot soak would relax her. She watched as the perfumed water foamed, and when the bubbles had almost reached the overflow drain, she peeled off her clothes and eased herself in.

She submerged as much of her body as she could, and since this was an old-fashioned tub perched on claw feet and twice the size of the modern variety, a good deal of her was underwater. She would dream a man, a perfect man—one who would come to her unencumbered by shadows and unreadable thoughts, yet still mysterious enough to be exciting. She closed her eyes with the effort, and what she saw was Karl eight years ago riding a bike, wearing a plaid shirt unbuttoned at the collar with the sleeves rolled up. He was crouched over the handlebars in accepted racing style, his hair blown back from his forehead by the wind. So vivid was the memory that she could see where the tanned skin of his cheeks became the lighter skin of his forehead, protected by his shock of sun-bleached hair. They had been flying along a narrow road somewhere north of Leicester where she'd lived. They were taking a long, straight downhill at breakneck speed. At the bottom it curved gently to the right and then flattened out to run alongside a shallow river. They had coasted to a stop and left the bicycles a few feet from the side of the pavement. On foot, they followed the shallow river for a short time, then left it to climb the side of the hill. It was heavily wooded with springy maple saplings that bent and gave when Christa pulled on them. Finally flopping down on a small round summit, they laughed, out of breath. The ground beneath them was hard but they made love on it, anyway. For a week afterward there was a small round bruise where a stone had dug into her shoulder—a reminder of their erotic encounter.

Christa sat up wearily in the tub and, reaching forward through the suds, tugged on the chain that held the plug. As the water gurgled out, Christa sat numbly until it had all drained away, then turned on the shower and rinsed herself. Wrapped in a thick terry towel, she padded across the apartment to her bedroom. Whatever charge had been pulsing through the rooms was gone. Moving slowly, weighed down by the past, she stepped into a flannel nightgown and buried herself in her bed. Covering her head with the quilt, she made herself invisible so that any random thoughts of Karl that might be flitting around the room would not be able to find her. Maybe tonight she would sleep.

THE REMAINDER OF THE WEEK passed slowly, and though Christa tried not to think about Karl, she was all too aware of him and what he might be doing. Was he eating lunch when she was, and restlessly trying to sleep through the same long nights? All day Friday, the thought that today he was coming back was her constant companion. *Not that I care*, she told herself sternly. *After all, I'm not going to see him again.* It was hard then for her to rationalize her wretchedness when by midnight he hadn't called.

Saturday morning poked into her bedroom with bright fingers of sun, energizing everything it touched. Christa woke with the nagging feeling that she'd heard something before she was fully awake. The ringing of the telephone shattered the morning and she sat bolt upright in bed. Throwing back the covers, Christa ran barefoot to the kitchen.

"Did I get you out of bed?" Karl's voice poured over her like warm syrup.

"Sort of," she admitted, ignoring the relief that oozed through her at the sound of his voice. The floor was freezing and she stood on one foot, placing the other against her shin in an effort to warm it.

"I apologize, but I got in too late to call last night. The sun is shining, the air is warm and I want to go to the beach. Will you come?"

He sounded so ordinary, as if calling her were the most natural thing in the world. Hadn't he felt the undercurrents running between them? She had a foreboding that if they continued to see each other something was going to surface, and with it a lot of pain for one or both of them.

"Isn't it too cold for the beach?" She parried for time.

"Today will be perfect. I'll pick you up in half an hour. Unless you have something else planned?"

Yes, yes she did. She had planned to reline the shelves of her cupboards and then she had planned to go to the library and get out some new books. And then she had planned to write a long-overdue letter to her parents. A full day. No room in it at all for a trip to the beach.

"Christa, are you there?"

"I'm here."

"Half an hour then?"

She should have the strength to say no. She tried, standing there with the telephone clutched in her hand, but the word would not come. "Half an hour," she said quietly and hung up the receiver.

The sun *was* warm. Karl had been right. Christa pushed the sleeves of her fleecy aqua exercise suit halfway up her arms. She felt pale and sickly in the bright sun. She'd be glad to be done with winter, glad to get out in the air and encourage some color in her skin. She squinted down the street, not knowing what she was looking for; she had no idea what kind of car he might be driving. There was no sign of a vehicle at all. What she did see was Elizabeth, who also saw her and waved. "Where've you been so early?"

Elizabeth waited until she was at the steps before answering. "I was out of coffee, so I went out to get some."

"Why didn't you come up? I have some."

"I did, but you didn't hear me. You were in the shower." Elizabeth took in the exercise suit, the sneakers with a black swoop on their sides, the ankle socks with small white balls bobbing in back. "Where are you going?"

"To the beach."

"No kidding? With whom?"

"Karl."

"Oh." Elizabeth kept her voice carefully neutral.

They both heard the engine at the same time and raised their eyes to look. The silver BMW cruised quietly between parked cars and came gracefully to a stop in front of them. Karl got out and, edging sideways between a jeep and an old Chevy convertible, walked to the stoop. Christa closed her eyes and took a deep breath as her heart rocketed around in her chest. He wore faded jeans that clung to his narrow hips like a second skin, and a navy-blue-and-white-striped sailor's shirt stretched tautly over his muscled shoulders. His sandy blond hair caught the sun and shone with golden highlights. Placing his foot on the step where she sat, he bent over to look at her closely.

"For a minute I thought you'd gone back to sleep." His blue eyes laughed under thick lashes.

"You're not wearing any socks," she said, thrilled by her brilliant comeback. Under the edge of his jeans she could see his bare ankles, the hair of his legs curling in fine gold spirals.

"I hate sand in my socks," he said, then looked up at Elizabeth and smiled. "I'm Karl von Klee."

"I'm sorry." Christa pulled herself together. "Elizabeth, this is Karl; Karl, this is my friend Elizabeth."

"And my mother refused to take part in the student exchange program. I may never forgive her."

He looked puzzled. "I think I missed something."

"Forget it," Elizabeth said. "I'm talking in circles. Don't let me hold you up, I know you have plans. But Christa, when you get home, give me a call? We have some things to talk about."

Karl held the door while Christa slid into the soft leather upholstery and then walked around to get in behind the wheel. He plucked his sunglasses from the visor where they hung, started the engine and they moved smoothly away.

"Didn't I tell you? The day is perfect."

She tore her gaze away from his sensitive fingers curved over the steering wheel, the nails well-shaped and clean, and looked out the window. The Saturday bustle hadn't started yet and the city streets were empty, lying quietly in the April sunlight that as yet had no substance to it. There was something pregnant about the scene, as if just around the corner something exciting were going to

happen. If only it *were* something good! If only today turned out to be as perfect as Karl claimed it
would be. Then it could become one of those nice
memories that people hoard as a protection against
sad times. Suddenly sadness was there in the car
with Christa, rubbing against her as soft and persis-
tent as a kitten. They were headed nowhere. A few
days spent together to fill in the time while Karl was
in Boston, and he would go back to Germany. And
the wound would be open again, raw and unhealed
as it had been before.

"Christa?" There was concern in his eyes.

She forced a smile. "Where are we going?" she
asked brightly.

"Let me surprise you," he said, his eyes still examining her with a trace of worry. "You looked so
funny there for a moment."

"I'm just not quite awake." Compelling some ani-
mation into her voice, she asked him about his trip.

"It went quite well," he replied, the tense line of
his shoulders melting a little. "Quite well."

FORTIFIED BY PANCAKES AND SAUSAGES they left the
city behind and drove north through the Massachusetts suburbs until they reached the coast at
the New Hampshire border. They followed the road
until it ended at a small marina.

Karl left the car and disappeared into a boxy
structure that had "North Shore Boat Basin"
painted in fading red letters over its doorway. A
fishy smell was in the air and the water made soft
swallowing sounds where it lapped against the

dock. In a moment he was back, moving the car around to a parking space at the side of the office. Christa climbed out warily and looked down the line of bobbing boats moored to a pier that stuck out into the shiny waters of a small cove like a weathered finger.

"Are we going fishing?" she asked cautiously. "Because if we are, I think you should know that I faint at the sight of worms."

"No fishing," he assured her, opening the trunk and handing her a blanket, a shopping bag and a wicker picnic basket. He slammed the trunk shut, took the bag and the basket and set off down the pier at a brisk pace.

They passed several large boats that Christa eyed with interest and stopped finally at a small motorized dinghy. Karl stepped gingerly into the boat, distributing their paraphernalia evenly over the gray wood bottom, and then reached out a hand to Christa.

"I'd prefer that one," she said, pointing to a trim sloop, its sails furled, its slender mast pointing skyward.

He stood impatiently, hand outstretched.

"This is an act of faith," she told him, grasping his fingers and balancing precariously in the bobbing craft before sitting down on one of the wooden planks that served as seats. A man followed them out on the pier and stood near the rope that held them securely to the dock.

"You sure you know how to run that?" he asked.

"I'm sure," Karl said with a scowl.

The man looked doubtful. "What time you think you'll be back?"

"No later than six," Karl replied.

"Ayuh, if you're not back by then I'll send the boys over for ya."

"Cast off for me, would you?" Karl called, and the man obligingly set the little boat free, tossing the rope to him.

"Good luck!" He waved to them as he started back down the pier, then he turned to ask, "You have enough gas?"

"The man must think I'm an idiot," Karl complained, not bothering to answer. "I've probably logged more hours in a boat than his entire family. Just don't make any sudden moves," he warned, as Christa twisted around to watch the dock recede.

It occurred to her that she had been in places where she'd felt safer. "I can swim," she offered disconsolately, "but I'd rather not."

"You won't have to," Karl assured her. Starting the motor, he aimed them out to sea.

Just free of the cove he veered right and headed for a small spot of land in the distance. The breeze was sweet with the smell of water and salt. It tugged at Christa's hair, blowing it in all directions. Above their heads two lazy gulls circled, grieving over the lack of anything substantial in their wake. Using both hands, Christa firmly pinned down the red-gold hair whipping around her face. "If I had known we were going to do this, I'd have worn a hat," she shouted.

"What?" he shouted back, furrowing his brow.

She waved her hand to indicate that it was nothing. Conversation was impossible over the sound of the engine.

The spot on the horizon grew rapidly into a tiny island with small houses on its highest point. Karl cut their speed, maneuvered expertly in to the small, ramshackle dock at the water's edge and shut off the ignition. He turned to smile at her. "Welcome to Bon Appétit." He secured the boat and lifted their gear onto the small dock. After climbing out himself, Karl reached a hand over to Christa to help her.

"What is this place?" she asked.

"It's a summer home belonging to the maître d' at the St. Pierre." He studied the house above them. "Primitive, isn't it?"

Christa laughed at the distaste in his voice. Her father, once he had learned something of Karl's background, liked to tease him about roughing it in Massachusetts. He had even threatened to take Karl camping, and for a while there had been a lot of talk about fishing lures and rifles and hunting permits. But the trip never came off. Christa suspected that for two brief years her father had had the son he'd always wanted. She'd been jealous of the male camaraderie that had existed between them—she could admit that now. She further suspected that her father still missed Karl and that Karl missed him. Karl never came to the States without driving up to Leicester to visit her parents; he had never visited her. The affection between the two men had added a dimension to her pain, which she had considered well-rounded enough as it was.

"Forward," Karl said. His eyes, which were his most arresting feature ordinarily, literally shone when he was happy. He picked up their supplies and advanced toward a haphazard flight of stairs that had been cut into the rocky shoreline, leading toward the house.

"Is it open?"

"No," Karl said over his shoulder, the wind disposing of his words so that Christa could hardly make them out. "They don't open the place until June."

"This is lunacy. We're going to erode."

"What happened to your sense of adventure?" he shouted, plodding on ahead of her. They reached the narrow plateau where the house sat and followed a faint path that led behind it. Up close, the building was an indiscriminate color, its shingles the shade of a rain puddle. With the cabin behind them, the wind was foiled. Christa sighed in relief and combed the tangled strands of hair back from her face.

The island swept out in a shallow crescent; they had docked at one of the pointed ends. To their right several feet below where they stood, a sandy beach smiled in a long half-circle. Four other houses were visible along its length, nesting patiently on the ridge under the brilliant blue of the sky. Stretched out before Christa and Karl, the ocean winked and flirted in the spring sunshine. It sighed against the beach, withdrew and sighed again. Some distance away, two figures stood at the water's edge fishing, while a dog and child ran in circles behind them. A sailboat moved serenely past, out beyond the quiet waves. Christa and Karl skittered down the ridge of dunes and spread their blanket on protected sand.

Christa raised her face to the sky and took a deep breath. Standing behind her, Karl placed his hands on her shoulders, his thumbs rubbing against the soft skin of her neck. "I remembered how you love the sea," he said.

"It's so sensible." She struggled to keep her voice steady. "It's just there doing what it's supposed to be doing. It makes whatever current dilemma I'm embroiled in seem less traumatic."

"It's hard for me to picture you traumatized," Karl confessed. "Even when you were younger it seemed to me you had things very well together. I felt sometimes as if I were falling apart, but you were steady as a rock."

"That was a difficult time for you, wasn't it?" she encouraged. Karl rarely talked of his feelings.

"It's never easy to lose someone you love. I'd been through it once when my mother died, but I was so young then it barely registered on me. I was totally responsible to my father—we had only each other here. For a while I blamed myself for what happened. Maybe I hadn't taken good enough care of him. I know," he said as she half turned to argue that statement, "I don't blame myself anymore. Your father helped me with that."

Professor von Klee's death had been Christa's first real brush with tragedy. No one had suspected how weak his heart was. She remembered Karl standing in the living room of her home, immaculately groomed, every hair in place, telling them that his father had died. Despite his calm demeanor, she'd had the impression that his clothing was all that held Karl together.

Her mother had offered him her condolences, distancing herself a little from his tragedy. He had smiled his appreciation, lips tight in his pale face. But her father had studied him for a moment and then embraced him, and Karl had caught himself just short of sobbing. "Mr. Monroe," he'd struggled to say, "this is very difficult."

"Yes," her father had answered. "You shouldn't have to go through it alone."

He'd flown back to Germany with Karl and stayed for the funeral. "It was strange," he said when they got back, "but I really felt I had to stay. Karl never said anything but it was as if there was the family and us, and if I had left it would have been Karl all by himself.

The sailboat was now directly opposite Karl and Christa. "That's nice," Karl said. "I'd like a boat like that."

"Where did you learn about boats?"

"You forget I grew up on a river."

"Is the Mosel big?" She couldn't imagine Karl boating in his own country.

"Big enough."

"Bigger than Fisher's Run?" she asked, naming the river that fed her parents' pond.

"Twenty times bigger than that." He put his arm around her shoulders and led her back to the blanket. *A perfectly normal gesture*, she told herself. After all, they weren't exactly strangers.

"There are families who live on barges on the Mosel," Karl said. "They never leave it. They make their living moving cargo up and down."

"How awful."

"No, you are wrong. It's a nice life. It always appealed to me. It seems so simple—your entire life defined by the size of your vessel. No trailing edges to get snagged. Of course—" and his voice had a note of resignation in it "—I have discovered through the years that nothing is really simple, no matter how it appears on the surface."

"What's it like living in a castle?" she suddenly wondered.

He folded his hands behind his head and lay back. "Interesting, lonely . . . expensive."

"Are there ghosts?"

"There's Marietta, she comes to haunt us frequently."

"Have you seen her?"

"I haven't the temperament to see ghosts."

"Why can't she rest?"

"She committed suicide. She hung herself with a Spanish shawl her unfaithful husband gave her as a birthday present. Karl Ernst von Klee, her husband, didn't like to be reminded of the tragedy, so he sent their little girl to live in Austria. They say Marietta comes back to look for her baby."

Christa studied him stretched out next to her, his eyes closed, his stomach rising and falling as he breathed. Such a sad story. Imagine having someone like Karl Ernst or Marietta in your history. Imagine knowing what your great-great-great-grandfather looked like. She and Karl came from different worlds, with different pasts, different futures.

"You're staring at me," he said without opening his eyes.

His voice made her jump. "Don't be so self-centered," she returned. She shifted her gaze to the house barely visible behind them. "Does your friend spend his summers here?"

"Part of them, probably."

"I would think after a day or two it would get rather lonely."

"It would depend on whom you had with you."

Her mind went careering off at the thought of the two of them alone on this island for a month. "The sun is really warm," she said, shaking away the mind pictures and unzipping her jacket to take it off.

"You'll get sunburned," he warned, eyeing her lazily.

"But not stripes." She dropped the straps of her tank top over her shoulders. "Now *you're* staring at *me*," she said without looking at him.

"I've missed you, Christa."

"You were only gone two days."

"I meant over the years."

"I have a hard time believing you gave me a second thought. Tell me about New York," she demanded, changing the subject.

"It was promising, nothing definite. Did you get in touch with the advertising firm?"

"They'll call you Monday." She narrowed her

eyes and examined the empty horizon. "What exactly was it about me that you missed over the years."

Down the narrow strip of beach the bark of a dog rose suddenly on the breeze and just as suddenly was gone. "I couldn't have married you," he said. "Even if I'd thought that's what you wanted. There was no way it would have been possible."

"Oh, I know that." She let some sand sift through her fingers. "What *did* you think I wanted?"

"I don't know that I thought about it at all. We were caught up in something that, by reason of who we were, was finite. It had a visible end. At some point I would go back to Germany and you would go on with a life that was so full I wondered sometimes that you had room in it for me."

She turned to look at him. "*You* were my life."

"No," he said softly, "only a part of it."

She turned back to the sparkling ocean. *Idiot,* she wanted to shout at him, *were you blind?* Maybe this was his defense, his way of rationalizing what he'd done, why he'd left her. "Was it hard when you got home?" She wasn't sure what information she was trying to elicit.

Karl sat up next to her. "It was very difficult. The whole management of the winery fell on my shoulders. But at least I was prepared for it. That was the reason for my years at Harvard."

That hadn't been what she was referring to but she abandoned her quest for more personal information. "Things were in pretty much of a mess when you got back, weren't they? I remember my father being concerned."

"Things had been in a mess for a long time," Karl confirmed. "My father was an academic, not a businessman. I think when he came to this country to teach, he was happy for the first time in his life."

"Had he taught in Germany at all?" She had assumed so, but Karl's words now indicated that might not have been the case.

"No." The word was curt. "The family felt it was beneath him. But when the opportunity at Salem came up, and I was going to be at Harvard, they felt it would be a good thing for all concerned. We might never have met." His smile was tentative. "Maybe you think that would have been better."

"Regardless of how everything else turned out, I liked your father. I wish I'd had the time to know him better."

Karl laughed deep in his chest, a low, private sound. "I think that's what's known as a left-handed compliment."

"As far as you're concerned," she said, arching her eyebrows and making her eyes wide, "it wasn't a compliment at all." She got to her feet quickly, dodging his hand as it reached for her, and started off at a slow run to the water's edge.

He caught up with her and they walked along wet sand packed hard as cement. "Are we friends?" He peered into her face.

"Don't be silly," she said, looking straight ahead. "We can't be friends, we used to be lovers."

"Then maybe that's what we'll have to be again."

She started to tell him what she thought of that idea, but he grabbed her hand and pulled her after

him, jogging toward the fishermen. They walked
the length of the island, and when they got back
Christa dropped gratefully on the blanket.

"That made me hungry. What's in the basket?"

"I have no idea. I called the kitchen and they
packed a lunch. Let's see." The wicker creaked as he
opened the lid. "Hmmm, not very inspired. It looks
like sandwiches and potato salad and pickles."

"Anything to drink?"

He looked insulted and held up two bottles of
wine. "What did you think of that wine I left for
you?" he asked, rummaging in the basket for
glasses.

"I haven't had a chance to taste it yet," she admitted.

"Tonight," he said sternly.

Christa sat up and crossed her legs Indian style,
spreading the napkin he handed her over them. The
turkey on rye sandwiches were wonderful. She had
a sneaking feeling that cardboard would have tasted
great. The wine was light and refreshing and icy
cold in its foam cooler. Draining her glass, she held
it out for more.

"Easy. This may look like water, but it isn't."
Karl carefully refilled her glass. "Do you remember
that picnic we had the night we went cycling and
ended up in some farmer's orchard stealing apples?"

"And the dog chased us?"

Everything he was feeling seemed suddenly concentrated in his eyes. "No matter what conclusions
you may have come to, I loved you, Christa."

The declaration caught her off guard and she

pressed her lips together against the sudden sting of tears in her eyes, hating him for what those words still did to her. "I thought we were going to forget...."

"There's a lot I don't want to forget. Do you remember that afternoon by the pond?"

"Yes, and I remember the time we climbed Mount Morris, and the night my parents went to Holyoke for the weekend, and the afternoon we spent on Horseneck Beach."

He reached out to touch her and she drew her arm back quickly.

"I remember other things too. An August afternoon when my father came home to say you had really gone—crying for weeks, months after that, waiting for letters that never came. Damn it, Karl!" She brushed the back of her hand across her eyes.

"I want you to understand what happened."

"Oh, I understand all right." She was suddenly very angry with him.

"No, you don't. You think you were the only one who got hurt? You think I left you that day and never thought about you again? Please, Christa, don't."

"I swore I would never shed another tear over you as long as I lived." He tilted her face so that she was looking at him. Her eyes spilled over and her mouth trembled. "Karl, I loved you so much."

He kissed her eyes, her cheeks and finally her mouth, his hands on her back strong and insistent. Oh, he was a magician, taking her ordinary collection of skin and bones, muscles and nerves, and turning them into something that shimmered and vibrated with energy. "Stop it!" She struggled out from his embrace and gasped as if she'd been drowning. "I can't go through this again. No, please, don't touch me."

"That's too much to ask. It's all I've thought of since that night at the St. Pierre—what it would be like to touch you again."

"Who do you think you are that you can waltz back into my life as if nothing had happened?" she asked desperately. She felt as if she were fighting for survival. "I will not let you use me again." She backed away from him.

"You think I used you?" His eyes held hers in a steady stare.

She wanted to say yes, wanted to fling the word at him, to give him the responsibility for her years of unhappiness, to make him bear the weight of it—but she couldn't. She knew it wasn't true. There had been much more to their relationship than that. "This isn't going to work," she said breathlessly. "I never should have called you. There's too much in our past for us ever to begin again."

"You're wrong. The problem is not our past, the problem is our future. Because you know as well as I do that whatever there was between us is still there."

"That doesn't change anything," she said, shaken because what he had pointed out was true.

"What are you doing?"

"Cleaning up." She stuffed the remains of their lunch back into the basket. There was no way she would spend one more minute on this beach.

He knelt beside her and held her arms still. "We haven't settled anything."

"Yes, we have." She wrenched free and jammed the bottle of wine back into its container. Grabbing the jacket of her exercise suit in one hand and the basket in the other, she lugged the basket across the sand, up the incline and over the dunes.

"Christa!" He shouted her name just once.

She plodded along the pathway, then down the steps to the dock. If he thought she was going to leave herself open to that kind of hurt again he was crazy. "And don't you start crying," she warned herself. She would be hurt, she had no doubt about that, because he was right—whatever had been there between them eight years ago was still there now, and nothing had changed. She'd fall in love with him all over again and he'd go back to Germany—back to that damn winery that meant more to him than anything else. For all she knew he had a wife in Einzell, someone who liked wine as much as he did. What chance did she have against that?

Her grand exit came to a dismal end at the dock. How like her to storm off in righteous indignation and then have to wait for the cause of her indignation to take pity on her and transport her home.

He came over the rise carrying the rest of their things. "You forgot your shoes," he said, dropping them next to her.

"Thank you." She forced them on and tried to ignore the abrasive sensation of trapped sand against the soles of her feet.

The drive back to Boston was filled with the tension of what lay unspoken between them. Finally, somewhere just inside the city boundary, he said, "I don't know how else to apologize to you. You think I had my fun and then went back to Einzell and put you out of my mind. That's not how it was. There were problems, things in my life that you knew nothing about. I did what I did because I had no choice. And I didn't answer your letters because there was nothing I could say to you. I was trapped by the situation."

"I've been trapped, too," she told him. "For years I've been trapped by your memory. All this time I've been trying to replace you with someone else, but I haven't been able to."

"Then why don't you stop trying? We're not children anymore. We can work something out."

"The cost is too high."

He made the turn into Claiborne Street and pulled up in front of her building.

"I wouldn't have called you, Christa. I felt too much responsibility about what happened to open the whole thing up again. Your parents kept telling me how happy you were, and I believed them. But you're not any happier than I am. Maybe we owe it to each other to see if what's missing in our lives is each other. I can't make you any promises, but I would like to see you again."

"Do you know what it would do to me to fall in love with you again?" she whispered.

"No," he said. "Do you?"

5

SHE LET HERSELF into the apartment and closed the door softly behind her, easing her feet out of her sandy shoes. The heavy silence of late Saturday afternoon hung over everything. Sitting on the edge of her bed, she studied the face that looked back at her from the shadowed mirror over her dresser. It was an attractive, intelligent face, now showing signs of sunburn. She wondered how such a face had become attached to an emotional system that lately spent so much time out of whack.

There was a sharp knock on her door and Elizabeth called, "I saw you come in, so open up." Reluctantly Christa let her in. Elizabeth walked directly toward the kitchen saying, "That's some old-friend-exchange-student you've got there. Mind if I make myself some coffee? And you sit right down and tell me all about that gorgeous man."

"It's a long story."

"I've got the time, my social secretary is holding my calls. Do you want some?" She held up a cup. Christa shook her head and looked away. "Hey," Elizabeth asked, "are you all right? Did he try something?"

"No, nothing like that."

She sat next to Christa. "You really are upset, aren't you? Do you want to talk about it? Who is this guy?"

"Someone I was in love with once, a long time ago."

"I thought there was more to this than you were willing to admit." She looked at Christa expectantly.

There was no way out of it. With a reluctant sigh, Christa began the story. "When I was sixteen years old, Karl's father came to teach at Mount Salem, the school where my father teaches. Karl's family owns a winery in Einzell, Germany, and his father ran it. There was some kind of trouble that ended with Karl and his father coming to the States. Karl went to Harvard to finish his M.B.A. and his father came to Mount Salem. Because my father taught German and my mother and I spoke it fairly well, Karl and his father used to visit and we got to be friends.

"Maybe I will have some coffee," she said, turning the heat back on under the kettle. She stared at the stove, then looked back at Elizabeth. "You've seen him. Can you imagine what it was like being in high school and having someone like that suddenly come into your life? And the thing is, he was wonderful—and lonely."

"A fatal combination," Elizabeth observed.

"We ended up spending a lot of time together. He wanted to know about my life. He had lived in the States for a while with his mother when he was younger. His parents were separated. I think it was a very bitter separation. When his mother died, he went back to his father in Germany. I always felt he was trying to find out what he'd missed. From what he told me, I got the impression the family in Germany was not very loving. He just kind of adopted ours." She measured instant coffee into her mug and covered it with boiling water. "We went bike riding, he took me to the movies, he helped me with my homework. It was as if I had acquired an older brother overnight."

"But not really," Elizabeth said.

"No, not really." Christa picked up the steaming mug and brought it to the table. "The first summer they went back to Germany, and I thought I would die. I missed Karl so much it scared me. When he came back it was as if I had permission to breathe again. I guess what I was feeling showed because our relationship changed. It looked the same on the surface—" she raised her eyes to look at Elizabeth "—but underneath it was different.

"Then his father died. It was an awful shock to everyone, especially Karl. I felt so badly for him and I was scared to death he'd go back to Germany. But he didn't. He had made some kind of promise to finish at Harvard, and he did.

"After his father was gone he practically moved in with us, and things between him and me got harder and harder to control. Then one day, after we'd been swimming in the pond behind our house, we became lovers." She stared at her cup, lost in her thoughts. Finally, she looked up. "At the end of the summer he went back to Germany, and except for two letters I never heard from him again."

"What a crummy thing to do."

Christa looked at Elizabeth quickly.

"You were a kid, Christa, he seduced you."

"No, that's not how it was." Her words were emphatic.

Elizabeth raised her eyebrows in disbelief, then let them drop. "What brought him back into your life?"

"Me. I called him. I got a letter from my mother saying he was in town and that he'd been asking about me. She thought it would be nice if I called him. I thought I was over him, or maybe I knew I wasn't. I don't know, but anyway I called him and here we are, right back where we were eight years ago."

"I take it something happened today on the beach?"

Christa went over their encounter in detail.

"Whew," Elizabeth said, leaning back in her chair. "Now what are you going to do?"

"I'm not going to see him again. I told him that."

"Why doesn't that surprise me?" Elizabeth asked the ceiling. ,

"Don't start on me." Christa warned, but Elizabeth chose to ignore her.

"As soon as things look like they might get serious, you back away. Don't look at me like that. In all the years I've known you, ever since we were wise enough not to room together in college, I've never known you to have a really deep relationship with a man."

"That's ridiculous," Christa said. "I didn't back

away from Karl, he left me. And what about Paul? Did you forget him?"

"No, I remember Paul. I remember thinking to myself that I would have been floating on air if I were in your place. You were as cool as lime sherbet, all your emotions nice and neat. And then when you decided you'd had enough, you kissed him, thanked him for some lovely times and sent him packing."

"You make me sound like an iceberg." Christa's words were touched with irritation.

"I don't mean to," Elizabeth denied, regarding Christa with troubled eyes, "because I don't think you are. You're a warm, wonderful friend, up to a point. There's some invisible boundary that you don't let anyone cross, not even me. You kind of glide through life, Christa—you don't get hung up on things. It's like you're oiled. Oh, Christa, I don't mean to hurt you."

Christa was looking at her, amazed. "You have no idea what you're talking about. You think because I don't run around all upset and disheveled, that things don't bother me? You think because I cope and don't fall apart, that I don't hurt? Would you like me to tell you how many nights I spent crying over Karl, how many mornings I woke up feeling desolate because I'd dreamed about him again, how many times I started each day with a prayer that this was the day I would hear from him?"

"Then why aren't you going to see him? You've got another chance."

"At what? I have no desire to go through that kind of pain again."

"You're not hurting now?"

"Yes, I'm hurting." Christa got up and walked angrily to the window, looking out at the web of clotheslines that bound the neighborhood together. "But I'll get over this."

"Maybe you shouldn't get over it," Elizabeth persisted. "Maybe you should give in to it. It's occurred to me over the years that you only let yourself get involved if you know from the beginning that the relationship has no future and you can call it off whenever you want." Christa remained looking out the window.

"This time you're not in the driver's seat. I think you're afraid to see Karl again, not because you think it won't work out but because you're scared it might. And if that's the case, things will be out of your control and you don't know how to handle that."

Christa closed her eyes against the memory of Karl's kiss on the beach. She had felt as if she were drowning, and had pushed him away, fighting for her life. "How *do* you handle it?" Her voice was thin and strained.

"You don't," Elizabeth said softly. "You just let it happen. You can't live life standing on the sidelines, joining the parade for a little while and then leaving it when things get tense. People need love," Elizabeth said. "They need to get it and they need to give it. . . . Giving it is almost more important. When my father died my mother got a cat. It was and is the most ill-tempered animal on the face of the earth. Does that bother my mother? Not at all. She thinks it's funny, she loves the stupid thing, and in the long run that's what's important.

"You've had all this feeling for Karl bottled up inside you for years, and now you're planning to put the cap back on it again. You tell me he's not a user, you think he has some real feelings for you. Maybe you should just let go and see what happens."

"Suppose he leaves me again?"

"Suppose he doesn't?"

Faintly, somewhere in the house a buzzer rang. Elizabeth started and looked over her shoulder at the clock on Christa's stove. "That's Mark." She buzzed him on the intercom. "Has anything I've said made any sense?"

Christa shrugged. "Some of it."

Elizabeth hesitated, her hand on the door. "Do you want to come down and eat with us?"

Christa shook her head.

"Are we still friends?" Elizabeth asked.

Christa smiled, surprised at how much the effort cost her. It was the second time that day someone had asked her that question.

CHRISTA HUDDLED in the corner of the couch, watching while the room deepened from lavender to gray, turning over and over in her mind the things Elizabeth had said. She had been angry, and Elizabeth had known it. The smile on her face as she watched Elizabeth close the door had not hidden that truth. But now, in the near dark, her feelings had changed.

The picture Elizabeth had painted of her was far different from the one Christa carried around. She knew there was a common theme running through her relationships. She had always assumed it was strength. The strength to walk away from what did not meet her expectations. The fact that no relationships ever did meet her standards, she had blamed on Karl. But what if the emotional thread that held her life together was fear, not strength, and Karl's memory was a convenient shadow to hide behind?

She closed her eyes and relived Karl's kiss, the pressure of his hand on her back. He would have taken her right there, on the beach with those fishermen a scant quarter of a mile away, she knew. It was his determination to have her that had begun her fighting for survival. Elizabeth didn't realize, she was too naive to understand, what it could cost to love someone like Karl. Christa was right to be afraid. Paul had put his faith in her, and he'd been wrong. How did you know when to trust?

You only get back what you give. That was one of her grandmother's sayings. Elizabeth had said almost the same thing, talking about her mother and the cat. There were parts of Christa missing, and Christa suspected Karl held them. Maybe the only way to be whole again was to give in to her feelings for him and let him bring her back to wholeness. She could deny it all she wanted, but the emotions he aroused in her were deep and powerful.

She got up from the couch and moved across the room, restless with desire. She wanted him, wanted to feel his lips on hers, his breath in her hair.

Elizabeth's footsteps sounded in the hall, then she rapped sharply at the door. Christa considered not answering, but after their talk, Elizabeth would worry. She padded softly to the door, opened it, and she stood face to face with Karl. He was still wearing the jeans and shirt he'd had on all day.

"Christa," he said with a wan smile, his face drawn and tired, "I did everything I could think of to keep from coming here tonight. I know you don't want to see me. I told myself that over and over, but as you can see it didn't make any difference—I came anyway. You're all I can think about. I can't get away from you. Please, can I come in?"

She backed away and let him pass, her mind filled with a mixture of distress and joy that he was here. He walked into the dim living room and sat tensely on the edge of the couch. "There's so much I want to tell you, and I don't know how. I guess in my heart I refused to admit how much I had hurt you. You see, I kept telling myself you would know that I was hurting, too."

"How would I know that, Karl?" she asked from where she stood in the doorway. "You never told me. Those few letters I got from you said nothing."

"I've never been very good at talking about my feelings, or writing about them either, for that matter. I couldn't imagine that after what we'd had together you wouldn't realize how much it would hurt me to leave you. Now that I look back on it I can see how you might have believed that my silence was lack of feeling, when in reality it was just the opposite. Christa, I knew I had hurt you and I hated myself, but there was nothing I could say to change what had to be. I couldn't bear to think of you or to think of what might have been." He sat quietly, hunched forward with his forearms resting on his knees. "So much of my life is a might-have-been, and that's really why I've come back." He looked at her leaning against the wall, slightly behind him. "I don't want this to end up that way, too. We've got another chance, and we're adults enough to deal with what that chance may mean. Maybe it will end up meaning nothing, but at least I won't spend the rest of my life asking myself if, had I done things differently, you might have loved me again. You can't tell me you have no feelings left for me because I won't believe it. There's something between us that doesn't need words. I can feel it now and so can you."

He got up and walked slowly to where she stood. "Tell me you don't feel it. Tell me I'm wrong, and I'll go."

"I can't," she whispered.

He bent slowly and placed his lips gently on hers. Her arms circled his neck. He remained still for a moment and then his arms tightened around her so she could feel the muscles of his shoulders bunching as his lips savaged hers. He pulled away and searched her face. "Christa?" The word was a plea for permission. Her heart was torn with divergent feelings, then she looked in Karl's eyes and was lost. Her hands cupped the back of his head, pressing him to her, holding him prisoner while passion rose in her, lifting her buoyantly, helplessly on its crest. There was one last moment of panic when fear almost overcame her, but she willed it away and allowed herself to be flooded by the sensations he aroused in her.

Karl slid his mouth along the curve of her throat, then kissed the back of her neck and the satin skin behind her ears. He breathed her name through the fiery strands of her hair. She arched her back so that the vital pulsing spot at the base of her throat was visible. Moaning her name, Karl pressed his mouth to it. Her blood beat under the warm, moist caress of his lips and coursed through her veins, the sound of its rushing filling her ears. There was no strength in any part of her. "Karl, Karl." It was almost a cry of desperation. "I've dreamed of this for half my life." He picked her up and cradled her so easily she might have been a child.

"There's no stopping this now," he said, his voice rough with passion.

"I know," she murmured against his mouth, not wanting to leave his lips for even a moment.

He started for her bedroom and she locked her arms around his neck, kissing him again, her tongue gently searching for his. He stopped, the intensity of their kiss forestalling any other movement. Then he broke away.

"Wait," he pleaded, his voice ragged. He brought her to her bed, and with hands shaking with impatience he pulled her soft cotton shirt roughly over her head and buried his face in her breasts. His tongue was a brand of fire where it touched her. "I've never had anyone I could give myself to," he whispered against her soft flesh. "There's never been anyone whose love I could trust. I want you to love me, I want to lose myself in loving you." He coaxed her into a response so exquisite it bordered on agony.

"Oh yes," she moaned. Her hands kneaded the muscles of his back.

Working impatiently at the buttons of his shirt he freed himself finally and tossed it away. He held her so that the warmth of their bodies met. "Can you feel it?" he asked, his voice a warm breath in her ear. "Can you feel the electricity between us?"

"I can feel it." She said the words joyfully.

His hands moved over her like a master musician, measuring and stroking every part until desire sang in her like a tightly wound violin string. The soft fleecy pants of her exercise suit dropped easily and he pushed them away. Blue eyes hooded under thick lashes took in her body. He drew a deep breath and traced the outline of her face. "How beautiful you are." His eyes darkened with mysterious thoughts. His fingers drifted across her lips, then moved quickly down the length of her body and passed lightly between her legs. She gasped and arched her back, her feet pressing into the soft down of the quilt. "What do you feel now, my love? Tell me so that I can be part of it, too." His hands lingered, touching her, but she was unable to reply. Christa sighed in disappointment when he stopped his tender probing, lifting her heavy lids to watch as he peeled the rest of his clothing from his body in sharp movements, flinging it to the floor. He stood over her, naked as she was, his lean body taut with excitement. He pulled her to her feet, molding her to him so that he pressed hard and throbbing against her. With enormous effort, as if passion had weight, she raised her head to look up into his face. His eyes flamed, his nostrils widened, she had been right to be afraid. What Karl wanted, what any man wanted, was her complete surrender. With others there had been no danger—she could keep a small distance between herself and them— but with Karl it was different. She felt herself drawn into his bottomless blue eyes. For one fleeting second she tried to surface, then gave it up as hopeless.

"Love me," he begged her. "Make me a part of you," and without releasing her lips, he pulled her with him until they lay on the braided rug. She did things she didn't know she was capable of doing, her hands moving over him, committing his body to memory. The spring of his muscles, the flat, firm span of his stomach—each plane and curve belonged to her now. She dug her fingers into his shoulders, needing to possess him, longing to be part of him too. His body was solid and unyielding, so unlike hers. She stroked the mat of rough hair on his chest, then sent her hand quickly along his throat, pausing to place her thumb on the pulse that beat in the soft hollow of his neck. It was like some primitive ritual, she felt. He had captured her life— now she would capture his.

He moaned, a deep animal sound, and lay with his eyes closed, head thrown back, his body a taut line. *"Liebchen,"* he breathed, "my *Liebchen.*"

Her lips skimmed his face, lingered on his closed eyes, then came to rest at his ears. With her tongue she examined the ridges and crevices she found there, while he shivered and said her name as if it were his mantra. In her heart an anthem swelled, the notes rising to a crescendo at finally being sounded after lying silent all these years. Her hand fled along the straining length of his body and she felt him quiver again. With a feeling of exultation she realized he'd been telling the truth. She had as much power over him as he did over her. As if reading her thoughts, his arms locked behind her with an iron strength. "You're mine," he said, "do you understand?"

He needn't have said it, there would never be anyone else after tonight; in truth there never had been. He reversed their positions so that she was under him. Heavy with desire he kissed her, searing her mouth, lifting her so far out of herself she was disoriented.

"My love." The words were a hoarse whisper against her cheek. She needed to be released from the fever that was raging inside her, and seeking some respite she raked her nails along the hard line of his back. He reacted immediately. His mouth crushed hers and he entered her in that sweet invasion that is both conquest and surrender. Arching to touch the body that was poised over her, she locked her legs around his and began moving rhythmically against him.

His features contorted as he struggled with a wild power beyond his ability to control. "Not yet," he said roughly, but it was too late. Taking the lead from her, he plunged them deeper and deeper into a shining darkness that exploded finally into a million shimmering pieces.

The shattered night fell softly around them and

then all was still. She cradled the back of his head and made little crooning noises to comfort him, to comfort both of them. They had been part of something frightening in its intensity. "My darling, my love, it's all right."

Something about her voice alerted him and he held himself up slightly to look at her. "You're crying," he said, startled.

"Am I?" She had difficulty saying the words.

"Did I hurt you?"

"No, oh, no," she sighed, brushing the hair from his forehead and smoothing it lovingly. "Nothing like that."

"What is it, then?"

How could she tell him that for all she had gained, she had lost something, too? She was not an individual any longer. She smiled shakily at the face above her, the face that had invaded her dreams and come between her and other men. His eyes held something now that they had never held before—a reflection of her, as she held a reflection of him. She had been right, he did hold the missing parts of her. He and she were separate beings who between them made a perfect whole. Separated, they would be nothing, a series of jagged edges like the old Hebrew mizpah coins that lovers broke in half, each one taking a piece and holding it until the time they were reunited, and the pieces joined to a perfect coin again. Her fear had a name now, it was called dependence.

How little it mattered that theirs might be a relationship without roots or foundation; a structure hurriedly erected when the time was right and just as quickly torn down and stored away. Life with only bits and pieces of Karl might be difficult, but life without him at all would be impossible.

"I love you," she said.

He gathered her close and she lay languid under him, stroking his back, his lithe, strong arms, the spare line of his hips. He sighed contentedly. Although she tried to ignore them, the hard ridges of the rug dug into her back, and not wanting to leave him, she tried to shift into a better position. Karl roused himself. "You can't be very comfortable."

"I'm not," she admitted reluctantly.

He rose from her slowly, pulling her with him until she was sitting up. Without the warmth of his body she shivered. Reaching behind them, he pulled the comforter from her bed and draped it around them, his arm under the quilt circling her back, his fingers grazing the edge of her breast.

She was satiated, filled to overflowing, and she leaned contentedly against him while he smoothed the hair back from her face with his chin and kissed her. Christa raised her lips to him and his mouth enveloped hers, his tongue lazily probing, his hands moving under the blanket to cup her breast. She was amazed to feel desire curling in her again. She had thought that wild, sweet hunger had been filled completely. She pulled back to find Karl smiling at her. "Later," he promised. "We have all the time in the world."

She surveyed the room, with articles of clothing strewed everywhere. Karl followed her gaze and

Succumb to
temptation ...

Could wealth, fame or power attract you to a man, even though you believe you love someone else?

This is just one of the temptations you'll find facing the women in new **Harlequin Temptation** love stories. Sensuous . . . contemporary . . . compelling . . . reflecting today's love relationships!

The passionate torment of a woman torn between two loves . . . the siren call of a career . . . the magnetic advances of an impetuous employer – nothing is left unexplored in this seductive new series from Harlequin. You'll thrill to a candid new frankness as men and women seek to form lasting relationships in the face of temptations that threaten true love. Begin with your FREE copy of **Uneasy Alliance**. Mail the reply card today!

Uneasy Alliance by Jayne Ann Krentz

He had a definite eye for beauty.

Meeting Torr Latimer was the last thing Abby Lyndon expected from her Japanese flower-arranging class. He was dynamic, good-looking, sexy – and he created much better floral arrangements than she did! He was also the distraction Abby needed in a time of crisis, for someone was stalking her . . .

Discovering her plight, Torr gallantly offered to protect her. He took Abby to his secluded cabin, where the atmosphere was intimate and safe – and conducive to seduction. Abby found all thoughts of the stranger menacing her melted away when Torr drew her yielding lips to his . . .

A word of warning to our regular readers: While Harlequin books are always in good taste, you'll find more sensuous writing in new Harlequin Temptation than in other Harlequin love stories.

Get this love story FREE
as your introduction to new

◀ See exciting details inside!

laughed softly. He lifted her onto his lap and tucked the quilt more securely around them. "You are a tigress," he said, resting his chin on her shoulder.

"I know," she said, a little embarrassed.

"You surprised me."

"I surprised myself."

"I've never experienced anything like that." His voice was joyous and he held her tightly, rocking back and forth. "It was magnificent, incomparable, stupendous. We have something very special." He tilted her chin so that she was looking directly at him. "It's been there since the first time I ever kissed you, waiting, all these years."

"Waiting," she whispered, "all these years."

6

CHRISTA BENT to retrieve her purse from the drawer of her office desk, slipped on the jacket of her mauve wool suit and flipped her hair up and out of her collar. On her way to the door she checked the mirror. Her eyes sparkled and her mouth curved in the perpetual half smile she seemed to wear these days. Opening the door she stepped out into the reception area.

"I'm lunching with the people from Lass Rollan," she told Katie Warren. "If Bob Fairfax gets here before I do, keep him happy."

"That won't be hard," Katie said, "we'll just trade innuendos while we wait."

"He's all bark," Christa said with a laugh.

"That's the trouble," Katie retorted as Christa headed for the elevators.

"Has it stopped raining?" she asked, hesitating at the office door.

"Don't know," Katie said. "You're the one with the window."

"That shows you how much time I have to look out."

On the street she breathed in the aroma of a city newly washed by an early spring shower. The three blocks to her appointment clicked by smartly under the assault of her navy-blue high heels; her arms swung in rhythm with her step. She was meeting Vera Eason. Vera was a decision-maker—shrewd, knowledgeable and impatient. She did not tolerate small talk. In that way she was a lot like Karl. Inane statements made Karl withdraw, if not physically then mentally.

Christa smiled at the thought of him, her whole body awash in a sensation of pleasure. She had only to think his name and his voice was in her ears, his hand on her back, his mouth against her lips. What would have happened if she and Elizabeth hadn't had their talk? It had taken courage for Elizabeth to do what she'd done. The morning following that conversation and Karl's arrival at Christa's apartment, Elizabeth had waited nervously for Christa.

"Is everything all right?" she'd asked.

And Christa had hugged her, a surprisingly spontaneous gesture, and said, "Everything's fine."

"Christa, I'm so glad. I'm the one who let Karl upstairs. He was coming in as Mark and I were going out, so I just held the door for him. I worried all night if I'd done the right thing. When we got home and his car was still there, I kind of hoped things had worked out."

"You know, I never even stopped to wonder how he got in without ringing the bell?"

"You mean I confessed for nothing?" They'd walked a few steps in silence and Elizabeth had asked, "And you're not mad at me? I really had no right to say all those things to you."

"You had every right; you're my friend," Christa had told her.

"Hey!" Christa felt a hand on her arm and looked up into the face of a policeman. She was teetering on the edge of the curb. "You try and cross now, lady, you'll get tire marks on that nice suit." He pulled her back to stand solidly on the sidewalk inches from traffic. "You have to stay alert in the city," he admonished her, and let go of her arm.

It was good advice. She couldn't spend all her time thinking about Karl. She forced her mind to focus on the meeting she was heading for. Meetings with Vera were apt to be prickly. Well, Christa doubted that Vera's sharp edges would bother her today. She felt eminently round and whole, a completely integrated unit. It would be hard to jar any part of her loose. By the time Christa reached Le Coq Bleu, her color was high and she was whistling softly under her breath. She really shouldn't still be handling Caldwell's dealings with Lass Rollan, Inc., but since she was just starting out and had few clients to take up her time, she was happy to help them out. It helped pay the bills. Besides, Vera Eason was a legend. There were only a handful of people who were able to get along with her, and Christa was one of them. She'd thought ruefully that if her consulting business showed signs of failure, she could make a decent living arranging things between Vera Eason and companies that wanted her business. She allowed Karl's smiling face to surface in her mind's eye one more time, blew it a soft kiss and went into the restaurant.

She glanced quickly at the inordinate amount of crystal visible and tried to forget that Martin Caldwell had what amounted to a small fit every time one of her luncheon bills with Lass Rollan came in. Following the maître d' to their table, she had barely been seated when a wraith of a woman approached. Looking at her, Christa wondered again how old she was. It was the best-kept secret in Boston. Her skin was flawless, which could have been makeup, and her face was wrinkle free, which could have been surgery; but her eyes seemed old. Christa had observed that you couldn't do much to a person's eyes to change them. They sat there for anyone to see, dutifully reflecting what went on inside that person. Christa experienced a totally unexpected wave of sympathy for Vera, as she expressed herself through those eyes.

"Ms Eason," Christa said, extending her hand, amused at the finishing school overtones her voice automatically took on when she was with her. Vera's handshake could only be described as bored. A waiter materialized and dutifully recorded her "very dry martini" and Christa's Perrier with a twist of lime.

Christa crossed her legs and sat back in her chair, taking her time, realizing that for all she complained about these meetings, there was something about Vera Eason she enjoyed. Once or twice she thought she caught a thread of something close to humor. Christa suspected Vera's reputation of being cold and difficult to deal with was simply a facade. And the fact that it worked—that it caused people to treat her with respect and a trace of awe—amused Vera. Christa was aware that Vera enjoyed meeting with her, too. The information they exchanged could have been passed over the telephone, but each time a decision had to be made, Vera suggested they meet for lunch here—at Caldwell's expense. "I hope the mock-ups arrived and that you've had enough time to examine them," Christa said.

"They came right on time, and as usual most of them are fine. I have just one or two small questions." Vera suggested some changes in wording that Christa had to admit improved the message the ad was trying to get across. The waiter returned and served their drinks, and they went on to discuss how Vera saw the future as it concerned Lass Rollan's association with Caldwell.

"Eventually, you understand, you will be dealing directly with them, or with Bob Fairfax," Christa said.

Vera eyed her coolly. "We'll see."

"What's that supposed to mean?" Christa asked, smiling.

"Bob Fairfax, to date, has not shown any great desire to handle me." Vera smiled cagily. "Maybe you'll decide there's enough money in the advertising end of things to stay with it. Getting started in your own business is not the easiest thing in the world. Being in business at all is difficult enough. Are you sure that's what you want to do?"

"Do you mean do I want to own my own business as opposed to working for someone else, or do you mean do I want to be in the business world at all?"

"Whichever question you'd like to answer."

"I want to do something with my life and working for someone else just doesn't fill the bill. I'm not interested in the corporate structure, and the small places don't offer enough room for advancement."

Vera cocked her head to one side. "I'm not sure that's a good enough reason to keep you going when times get rough. And they will. If you had said you wanted power, or there was something inside you that cried out to be fulfilled by helping small businesses improve their image, I might feel a little more confident. But we'll see. I've been wrong before. Who else do you handle besides Caldwell?"

Christa hesitated. The other firms she had dealt with had needed limited help, nothing on the scale of Caldwell. "Don't be afraid to say no one," Vera said. "It's no crime to be small, just to be stupid, and you are anything but that."

"This is my first big account," Christa admitted. "But I am doing some work with a German wine manufacturer, although that's more on the basis of friendship than business."

Vera raised her eyebrows. "Would it take much to change it into business?"

"I think so," Christa said, "more than either my friend or myself would be willing to give."

"Aha, it's *that* kind of relationship. Well, my dear, watch yourself. It's an Eason law never to mix business with friendship. It doesn't work. Ever. Don't stare at me like that, I know what you're thinking. You're saying to yourself 'what does she know, since it's universally believed that Vera

Eason has no friends.'" And then the sharp lines of Vera's intelligent face altered themselves into a broad wink. "Which just goes to show you how little the world knows."

Christa laughed. "I didn't believe that anyway. I like you very much."

"I know you do," Vera said. "And I like you. More than that, I've got respect for you. You've chosen a rough road to follow, you can't afford too many mistakes."

"Did you find it hard, being a woman?"

"In business? Not really. I don't think it would have been any easier for me if I had been a man. It takes the same things to succeed whether you're a man or a woman. Single-mindedness, ruthlessness, a willingness to work twenty-hours a day and the ability to give up everything else. Plus an absolute need to get what you're going after. Do you know how many people have that combination? How many people really mean it when they say they want to win?"

"Not many," Christa admitted.

"Damn few," Vera said. "Now if you'd like to know if I find it hard being a woman with a personal life when I'm also an executive in business, that would be another story. The answer to that one would be yes. You'll find, my sweet, that a woman is called on to make any number of difficult choices that a man will never face. Some of them are put on her by society, and some of them by herself, because she's a woman, because she has needs and desires most men never have to come to grips with. But don't let that discourage you. Problems have solutions." She paused while the waiter took their order for lunch and then said, "I know of a business that could use your services." She gave Christa the name of a firm that made expensive silver and porcelain buttons.

The rest of the lunch passed in informative conversation touching on the Boston business community. As was her custom Vera refused dessert, swallowed the last of her coffee, tapped her mouth with her napkin and said goodbye. "Remember," she cautioned, "if things go wrong, you always have an out. You can find some wealthy man to marry, have a few children and let the rest of the world go by." She waited to see what Christa's reaction to that would be.

"Is that what you plan to do?" Christa asked.

Vera smiled, her eyes telling Christa that for her a life without challenge or power would be no life at all. Christa watched her thread her way through the tables, stopping once to exchange a few words with someone she knew, her shoulders slouched, her hip thrust out at a sharp angle. She wondered what it would be like to have the kind of power Vera Eason had. She wondered if there would be a man anywhere foolish enough to be drawn to that icy resolve. She supposed there was, but had to wonder what kind of man would be willing to play second fiddle to Lass Rollan, Inc. for the pleasure of sharing Vera's life.

COMPARED TO THE ACTIVITIES the day had held, the night in its turn was quiet. It had cleared and stayed warm and the air held a spring sweetness. Christa and Karl drifted slowly through the old Boston Common; the lamps were lit and couples passed them, lingering as they did.

They had eaten in Karl's rooms and then decided on a walk. Christa hooked her arm through his, enjoying the look of her pale mauve wool against the rough tweed of his jacket. Shivering a little, she hugged his arm closer.

"Are you cold?"

"Just a bit." She hated to turn and go home. He took off his jacket and hung it around her shoulders. It reached halfway to her knees and the sight of her made him laugh.

"You look like someone playing grown-up," he said and carefully buttoned the jacket so that it wouldn't slip off.

She plunged her arms into the sleeves and linked elbows with him again, and they continued their meandering walk like a contented old couple, Christa thought serenely.

"In Germany the weather isn't so changeable," Karl said. "About the beginning of April the days get warm and they stay that way. For weeks at a time the temperature hardly varies more than a degree or two. It rains, it doesn't rain, that's the sum of the changes. But here!" The frustration in his voice made her smile. "I have to go outside and walk around the block each morning to determine what clothes to wear. And even that is only a partial solution because what's fine in the morning is totally unsatisfactory by afternoon. No wonder Americans are so volatile."

"You like us volatile and you know it."

"You're absolutely right." He grinned, dropping a kiss on her nose.

"I got a call from my mother today," she said. "She thinks it's nice that we've been able to spend some time together."

"What would your parents say if they knew what kind of time we spend together?"

"I think they would be pleased."

"But you haven't told them?"

"No." What she and Karl had was too fragile to risk sharing with her parents. She still thought of it as something of a miracle. And the knowledge that someday he would have to go back to Germany lent their love an air of poignancy. She wanted to keep what they had to herself.

They started across the bridge spanning the pond where swan boats glided on hot summer days, and they paused to look into the water, their arms resting on the rough cement. Christa glanced at Karl. He was staring at the water, his hair ruffling slightly in the breeze, his eyes focused on something that was not part of the scene in front of them. The thought came to her that there was a Karl she knew nothing about, whose life in Germany was, and probably always would remain, a mystery to her.

"What are you thinking about?" she asked him.

He turned to smile at her. "I was thinking how much I love you."

"No, you weren't. What was it?"

He looked back over the water. "When I was a

child, my father and I would go down to the river almost every night. We would feed the swans, and I would throw stones to watch the ripples. Sometimes we would see a barge and pretend we were on it, sailing away somewhere." There was a note in his voice that made Christa's heart ache.

"Do you miss your father still?"

"Do I miss him?" Karl asked himself the question. "I don't know. Sometimes I think I miss what could have been more than what really was."

"Your childhood wasn't happy, was it?"

"Everything is relative. At the time I thought it was normal. Later I blamed my parents, but I shouldn't have. They were caught up in the tragedy as much as I was."

"What tragedy?"

"It was not a happy marriage. My aunts and uncles never approved of my father's choice of a wife. And my mother was not happy living in Germany."

"It must have been hard for your father when she brought you to live in the States. I'm surprised he let you go."

"He didn't find out about it until it was an accomplished fact."

"She kidnapped you?" Christa asked, shocked.

"My little one," he said, kissing her on the forehead, "not everything is so black and white you can put a name to it. Why are we spoiling this beautiful night by talking about something that happened a long time ago and was very sad and is probably better left forgotten?"

She wondered how much of it he had forgotten, and how much it had colored the rest of his life. Was that why he'd been so unconnected, his ties to his family so nebulous? She remembered again her father's comments when he'd returned from the professor's funeral—how he felt he had to stay, that without him Karl would have had no one. Even Karl's relationship with his father, which seemed the strongest of all his relationships, had a flaw in it that she hadn't been able to quite put her finger on. Maybe the reason he'd been able to leave her the first time was that he'd never really understood commitment.

How much have you learned since then, Christa silently asked his sculptured profile. Aloud, she asked, "Why didn't your mother like Germany?"

"I think it was my father she didn't like."

"Oh, Karl," she said softly, "then she was wrong. The professor was a lovely man."

He shrugged. "You knew him when he was happy. The year he spent teaching at Mount Salem was probably the happiest of his life."

"Did you love him?"

"So many questions."

"He loved you."

"Oh? And how did you determine that?"

"I could tell."

"He sometimes had a strange way of showing it."

"Did you love your mother?"

Karl was quiet for so long Christa thought he wasn't going to answer her. "I know that for you that's a simple question. If I'd had your parents my answer would have been simple, too. But my parents were nothing like yours, and my family is nothing like yours. They are an old-world German family, stiff with tradition and rigid ideas of what is right and what is wrong. My parents made mistakes, and with the von Klees mistakes last a long time. Because of those mistakes my life has been very hard for me in many ways."

"What happened?" Christa asked softly.

"It's a long story, and someday I'll tell it to you. But not tonight, *Liebchen*. No more about the past tonight." He took her arm and they started walking again, their feet making sharp sounds on the gravel path. Christa watched their shadows retreat, then advance as they passed under a light. "I saw Bob Fairfax today," Karl said, moving the conversation to less painful ground. "He had some interesting ad ideas to show me. I have them back at the hotel. I'd like you to look at them." He increased his pace. "I'm getting cold," he complained.

"I bet you think I'm going to be self-sacrificing and give this jacket back," she said, "but I'm not. If one of us has to be cold, I'd prefer it was you."

"You'll pay for that," he said. "When we get back it will be your responsibility to warm me up."

"My pleasure," she said demurely, wanting a chance to take the sadness out of his eyes.

"No," he said, breaking into a jog and pulling her along with him, "I think it will be mine."

They ran the last few blocks to the St. Pierre, and by the time they were in the elevator they were out of breath. He kissed her—a long sweet kiss—and she broke away laughing. "I can't breathe."

He glanced at the indicator. "You have five floors in which to recover."

"I'd give my right arm for a cup of coffee," she said as he unlocked his front door, "but I suppose you don't have anything but champagne?"

"You complain about the damnedest things." Karl moved toward the small kitchenette. "Anything else?"

She switched the radio on and a piano concerto mingled with the muffled, faraway sound of engines and horns. The muted noise of traffic was a constant in the room, like the surf at the shore. Sitting on the love seat, Christa draped her arm along its back and waited for Karl. Finally, he sat next to her, his legs straight out in front of him, his head thrown back to rest near her hand. Turning slightly, he pressed his lips to her fingers. She was amused at his posture. Given a chance this was the way he always sat, stretched out as if there were no chair big enough to hold him.

"Let me see the ads," she said.

He dragged himself up and came back with a large portfolio. It contained several roughed-in drawings, which he spread out on the coffee table. They all had a misty, dreamy quality. Christa inched forward to look at them.

"What do you think?"

"He seems to have come down rather heavily on the romance angle. Of course that's one of your strongest selling points. I like this one." She pointed at a sketch in shades of lavender and pale gray. It showed a castle, set on a hill and surrounded by vineyards, rising out of the mist. Drawn so faintly they were just visible were the figures of two men in Roman togas, examining the grapes. The copy read: "We've been perfecting our wine for nine hundred years. Isn't it time you tried some?"

"You don't think it's too much?"

Christa glanced up at the note of uncertainty in Karl's voice. "No, not at all."

"That's the one I liked but I wasn't sure. I don't know enough about this. I feel off balance," Karl admitted.

"What did Bob say?"

"He liked that one and this one." Karl pointed to another board.

"You can trust his judgment—he's pretty sharp," counseled Christa.

"So you'd go with this one." He returned to the picture of the castle.

"Yes, if you're asking my personal preference. If you're asking me to give a professional judgment, I'd have to hedge. I haven't done any research on the demographics of wine lovers. But just off the top of my head, I can't see anything detrimental in that ad."

He studied it quietly.

"Are you the last word?" Christa asked. "I mean, can you make the final decision or do you have to check it through with someone else?"

"I don't know," Karl said. "It depends on what happens when I get back. If I can get them to agree to advertise at all, then I suppose they will leave the choice of what to use in my hands. And I'm not at all comfortable with that responsibility." The kettle whistled and he walked back to the kitchenette. "However, I suppose it's an area that I can learn about if I put in some time."

Christa cleared the ads away, leaving just the one propped up where they could see it. Karl put two steaming mugs of coffee down on the table, then stood with his hands sunk into his pockets, studying the ad board. "That one," he said again. "You agree?"

"I agree," Christa said uneasily, wondering if there was more to his questioning than appeared on the surface. Was he asking her opinion as a friend, or was he looking for some deeper involvement on her part? The possibility that he might be asking her for a professional opinion was an exciting, flattering thought. Before she could pursue it further, Karl sat next to her and draped his arm over her shoulder.

"It's a relief to have someone to talk to," he said, looking somewhat anxious. They sat that way for a moment, then he got up and walked to the window. He had been edgy all evening—somehow removed from whatever was going on. She watched him now, his hands on either side of the window looking down into the street.

"If you don't like these ads, you don't have to use them. You're not committed, you know—there are other agencies." It might be better for both of them if he saw someone she had never been connected with.

He looked rather surprised, then said, "No, the ads are fine. I think they'll be all right."

She waited for him to go on, to tell her what was bothering him, but he remained silent. A small knot of fear began to form in her stomach. "Come and sit down," she invited, not wanting to hear whatever it was he was going to say. "I have a duty to perform, remember? I can't warm you up long distance."

He turned and rested his back against the window. "I have something to tell you."

The knot tied itself tight with a wrench.

"I've put this off and put it off, waiting for the right time, and now there's no time left. I have to go back to Germany."

Everything was as it had been a moment ago. The coffee steamed silently, music curled around the fringes of the room, but inside Christa a clock had stopped. Still, it wasn't as bad as she was afraid it was going to be. What had she thought he was going to tell her? That he had been mistaken, that what he'd thought were deep feelings for her had turned out to be less than that? In her heart she had always known that he would be going back, so to hear him actually say the words was almost an anti-climax. "When?" She searched his face.

"As soon as possible." Her eyes slipped past him and fastened unseeing on a picture that hung on the wall to his left. Karl waited for her to say something and when she didn't, he went on. "Wilhelm Tietjen, our wine broker, is coming and I have to be there when he arrives. Even if he weren't coming I'd have to go back. I've been gone too long."

"Well, it's not as if I didn't expect it."

He studied her as if he were trying to gauge something, then said, "Come with me. Before you answer, listen. I know how you feel about the winery but that's because you have no idea what it is I'm fighting to preserve. I can tell you about it and you can think you understand, but you really don't. I want you to come to Einzell and see for yourself. I want you to see the castle and the river and the vineyards. I want them to mean something to you."

Christa was overwhelmed. Go to Einzell with Karl? "And then what?" she managed.

"And then we'll have to have a very serious talk. I love you, Christa, you must know that, but I'll tell you anyway so that we don't have any more misunderstandings. I think I've loved you since the first time we met."

And Christa knew she loved him. But for all her life, the part of it that mattered, Einzell and all the word stood for had been her enemy. Now Karl wanted her to know it and love it because there was no way he would ever leave it. If she wanted him, she would have to accept it along with Karl. "Do you have any idea of what you're asking?" she asked softly.

He came across the room and took her in his arms. She stood quietly against him, her head on his chest, every beat of his heart driving home to her the enormity of what was happening. "I know what I'm asking. If I had a choice, I wouldn't ask it."

"You do have a choice, Karl," she reminded him firmly. "You don't have to go back. They don't own you."

He laughed without humor. "No, they might even be relieved if I didn't come back. I'm returning because *I* have to." He cupped her face in his hands. "We have something, you and I. People who are very lucky find this kind of thing once in their lifetime. We've stumbled on it twice. The first time I made a mess of it. I don't want to do that again."

She had no doubt that he loved her. His eyes, those mirrors of the truth, told her that, and she knew what she felt for him. "Come back home with me, Christa."

It seemed strange to her that he could refer to that place as home. She seemed to have lost hers. It wasn't the apartment on Claiborne Street anymore, and for years it hadn't been the small Cape Cod where she had grown up. The only home she had these days was the one Karl offered her—the incomparable shelter of his arms and the warmth and comfort of his body, whether it was in Boston or in Einzell.

7

THE SMALL LANCET WINDOW set deep into the thick exterior wall of the castle was slightly ajar. A faint hum of activity came from outside. Christa tossed back the covers and walked across pale blue carpeting to push the window all the way open. Below in the narrow street, a group of children moved along in a tangled knot. Several yards behind them walked an older couple in their Sunday best. They carried on a conversation with a young man riding a bicycle in a weaving pattern to keep pace with them. Christa watched as the walkers passed beneath her on their way to St. Martin's.

It was just past seven o'clock and the street was still in shadow. The bell in the old church had wakened her this morning as it had every morning since her arrival in Einzell, ringing for two minutes, then swinging slowly silent so that the last sounds were more imagined than heard. A boy from the village rang the bell every morning and evening at six o'clock rousing the village, then calling it home again.

Christa glanced from the street to the houses that lined it and to the mountain that formed their backdrop. Veiled by a thin haze, it had the same soft,

early-morning look she'd seen on the hills at home.
Early morning in Germany was much like early
morning in Leicester, Massachusetts. There was
something about light, and smell too, that told the
time so effectively. Mornings didn't smell the same
as evenings, and April didn't smell the same as
August.

Resting her chin on her hand, Christa gazed at the
hill, void of trees but bristling with poles and spiky
vegetation. In her wildest imagination she would
not have pictured vineyards looking like this. The
only other grapevine she had ever seen was a lush,
tangled, friendly affair in the backyard of one of her
friends.

She had first seen the von Klee vineyards when
Karl drove her from the airport to the castle. The
hills on both sides of the placid river were covered
with an army of poles, each supporting two loops
of vine, like wiry hearts festooned with green
leaves. The vines gave the place a wild, unshaven
look and left her with troubled feelings she had not
been able to define. Now suddenly she knew. The
vines had been there when Roman legions camped
in the hills. *They make me feel insignificant*, she
thought. *Totally unimportant*. She crossed the
room again and crept back under the covers.

In the shimmering morning light the rough pink
plaster walls and ceiling of the ancient room glowed.
Christa glanced behind her at the ornately carved
headboard. This had been Marietta's bed—Marietta
of the lost child and lethal Spanish shawl.

"There are no ghosts." She said the words aloud,

reassuring herself that at least there was none of the kind Karl had hinted at. Closing her eyes, she conjured up the only image she had any interest in—Karl's smiling face. He had been so glad to see her, stalking impatiently on the far side of the Customs area, swinging her in a hug that lifted her off her feet when she finally came through, kissing away the memory of the ten days that had separated them.

She sighed at how deeply they were involved, how silly she had been to think she had a choice about coming. Ian Caldwell hadn't been pleased about her leaving, and her initial thought had been, *If it looks as if I'm going to leave him with unfinished business, I won't go.* Christa wasn't about to jeopardize the reputation she had worked so hard to build and that was just now beginning to show results. Karl had his business to worry about and so did she.

But he hadn't been gone twenty-four hours when she realized how "independent" she really was. She missed him desperately, and his absence brought back sharp memories of how it had been for her once before. Karl had become the background against which she lived her days.

His Aunt Edythe had greeted Christa cordially, thanking her, though she admitted it was many years past due, for the friendship the Monroes had extended to Karl and his father during their years in the States. "I am happy that we finally have the opportunity to repay that kindness. I think there is much that you will find interesting here." She spoke faultless English in a formal, slightly stilted way. Christa wondered if her own German had that same odd quality. There was nothing she could put her finger on, but she had the feeling that Edythe's welcome was not overwhelmingly friendly. Christa had asked Karl, suggesting that perhaps it was simply Edythe's difficulty with the language that had given her that impression.

"My aunt is not an effusive person, so don't expect that she will give you the same type of welcome your mother gave me. It just isn't in her to do that. But she truly is glad you're here. She meant it when she said she was grateful for what your family did for us."

Now Christa glanced at her small quartz alarm and noted that if she didn't hurry she would be late for breakfast. Things were done on schedule here.

Once showered and dressed, she descended the circular stairs, housed in one of the towers flanking the castle's front door. After being in the dark corridor, she found the stairs bright with daylight slanting in through glass-enclosed weapon slits. Christa entered the reception area and suffered the scrutiny of ancestral eyes gazing at her from gilt-framed portraits, while she listened intently to the undercurrent of voices from the dining room. But strain as she might, she couldn't pick out Karl's. Praying she would find him there, she squared her shoulders and walked across the uneven stone floor, pausing in the dining-room doorway.

Karl was there, deep in conversation with Edythe. She sat facing away from Christa, her pale hair swept back and fastened into a tight knot at the base of her skull. Her features were a vague echo of Karl's, less defined yet at the same time harder. She and Vera Eason would make an interesting pair, thought Christa. Then Karl saw her in the doorway. Blotting his mouth with a linen napkin, he began to rise.

"Don't stand up," she said, entering the room.

"Good morning," Edythe said in English, a smile breaking the contours of her face but not quite lighting her eyes. "I hope you slept well."

"Very well, thank you."

Karl pulled out the chair next to his. "I didn't think we would see you quite this early."

"There's so much to see and I don't want to miss any of it," Christa explained, flashing a smile at Edythe.

"You might want to select something to eat before you sit down," Edythe suggested. "We serve ourselves on Sunday. It makes things easier for the kitchen. You are right to want to fit in as much as possible today. Once Monday comes Karl will have his hands full with all the things that have been waiting for him." Then she switched to German. "Make sure there are enough eggs," she said to Karl.

"There are," Christa answered her. She wondered if Edythe had any idea what their relationship was, and if she disapproved and blamed Christa for keeping Karl so long in Boston.

Edythe laughed quietly, "I forgot you speak German. I'll have to watch myself."

Christa smiled at her and, holding back her natural inclination toward complete and instant friendship, kept the smile from lighting her eyes, too. "Your English is wonderful." She came back to the table, her plate laden.

"Your German is also quite remarkable."

"Thank you. I find I have no trouble with it grammatically, but emotionally it's often inadequate."

"It may not be your German that's at fault."

"Stephan!" Edythe swung around in her chair to greet a tall, dark-haired young man. He could have been Karl's dark twin, but he was younger, with brown eyes instead of blue.

"The emotions in this household are sometimes difficult to follow. Good morning, mother," he said, dropping a light kiss on Edythe's cheek.

"I didn't know you had arrived." Edythe reached up to pat him and this time the smile on her face reached all her features.

"Late last night." His eyes traveled around the table and stopped at Christa. He stretched his hand out to her. "Stephan Schröder."

"Christa Monroe," she answered, as he gave her hand a single firm shake.

He picked up a plate and walked to the buffet. "The American," he said, pausing to choose between several types of cheese.

"How was your trip?" Karl asked.

"Uneventful. The roads between here and Luxembourg are not a challenge at this time of year."

Edythe shook her head at her son. "Your affinity for ice and snowslides has never been understandable to me."

"Ah, there's a great deal of excitement in navigating tricky terrain. Don't you think so, Karl?"

Christa saw Karl's hand grip his fork. Obviously the question involved more than dangerous roads. She glanced up at Stephan and met his eyes, hard and unreadable. There was none of the vulnerability she often surprised in Karl's. Stephan held her look and then smiled. "You're older than I had been led to believe." Flustered, Christa could think of nothing to say. "That was a compliment," he told her. "My cousin has always referred to you as a schoolgirl. I'm pleased to see that you're much more than that."

Alongside her own, she felt the muscles of Karl's leg tighten into hard knots. She stole a glance at him, but his face was composed. Stephan settled himself at one end of the table, spread his napkin over his knees and speared a piece of sausage.

"Yvette isn't here?" he asked no one in particular.

"Neither is Marcel," Edythe replied. "Mademoiselle Chenard sends you a message. She advises you to be patient."

"It's my greatest asset," Stephan said, and looked around for someone to contradict him.

"Since it's his daughter you seem to have your eye on, Marcel will be happy to hear that," Karl said dryly.

"Yvette knows what's at stake. She's willing to bide her time."

"I'll bet she is," Karl's voice was hard.

Edythe shot him a glance and Stephan, catching her look, changed the subject. "How was your trip, Karl?"

"Interesting." Karl's voice had lost its edge and was casual, surprising Christa, since the rest of him seemed wound tighter than a watch spring. He must have had years of practice hiding his feelings, he did it so well. "I'll hold my information until the wine broker arrives."

"Have you spoken to Wilhelm? When is he due?"

"Soon."

Stephan took a great deal of care buttering his roll. "I can hardly wait," he said dryly.

"Are you finished?" The abruptness of Karl's question took Christa by surprise. Glancing down at her still-full plate, she shrugged. "Then I think we'll be going." He rose from his seat. "If you'll excuse us?"

"Miss Monroe has barely touched her breakfast," Stephan observed.

"It's all right," Christa assured him. "I took too much."

"I understand Karl is going to show you the vineyards," Edythe broke in. Christa had the distinct impression she spent a good deal of her time heading off confrontations between Karl and Stephan. "You'll find them quite different from anything in Massachusetts."

"You've been to New England?" Christa asked.

"When Karl's mother died."

"I don't imagine you had a chance then to see much."

"No. It was far from a pleasure trip. Someday I'd like to go back. Enjoy your morning," she said abruptly, dismissing them.

They left the castle by the front door, cut across the cobblestone courtyard, where Stephan's small red Mercedes was parked, and continued through the gardens. At one time they must have been lovely, but now they were untended and overgrown.

Karl hurried Christa along, taking long, hard steps as if he were punishing the ground. The sun electrified his blond hair and bleached the color from the blue of his chambray work shirt. Looking up at him, Christa experienced a dizzying feeling of possession. She knew what his body looked like beneath those clothes, what the skin of his shoulders felt like, and she knew too how upset he was, though she was confused as to why.

It had something to do with Stephan. Perhaps it was an old anger and went back to when they were children. She had seen how fondly Edythe had looked at her son and a sensitive ten-year-old who had just lost his mother would have been sure to feel somewhat left out. Karl had mentioned Stephan to Christa offhandedly on several occasions. It was obvious to her now that he held a place in Karl's life that was much more important than Karl had ever admitted. But the morning lay like a warm blanket across her shoulders, too beautiful to let anything spoil it. She would ask Karl about Stephan later, when they were alone and he had calmed down.

She stopped abruptly and grabbed his arm, forcing him to stop, too. "You haven't said a word about my outfit, and I chose it especially for our morning," she pouted playfully.

Karl looked at her. Christa was wearing purple

slacks and a lavender knit shirt, her hair hanging loose around her shoulders.

"The pants," she teased, holding them away from her legs when he seemed puzzled by her statement. "Grape color . . . vineyards?"

A smile crept across his face, and he shook his head. "How stupid of me, I should have realized. Except, of course, the grapes we grow are white."

"It took me half an hour to decide on these," she mourned in mock dismay.

Karl's expression lightened and he hugged her quickly.

"You look wonderful, darling. You light up my existence here in Einzell." He hurried her down a flight of stone steps. She waited while he unlocked a thick wooden door with iron hinges as big around as her wrist. It opened soundlessly into a small stone room. Karl pulled a hanging oil lamp down and lit it before he shut the door behind them. The room was very cold.

Then, he pulled her to him in a fierce hug and kissed her thoroughly, taking his time, doing things he knew she would respond to. The sensations he always evoked in her began their slow seduction of her body. "Good morning," he said, finally. "I've been wanting to do that for an hour."

"She locked her hands behind his back and leaned away from him. "Then why didn't you?"

"I'm protecting your reputation, remember?"

"Well, I hope all this protection doesn't get one of us killed. Every time I hear you outside on that balcony it makes me nervous. Actually it would probably kill both of us if you fell. I'd have a heart attack."

She was talking about the method Karl used to get to her room. He claimed it was because he wanted to avoid the more public halls and stairways where he might be seen coming and going. Christa suspected it was because he considered it more romantic, not to mention more convenient. A small door in the corner of her room, hardly more than eighteen inches wide, opened onto a narrow balcony tucked into the roofs and turrets of the castle. The door had to be raised by a jacklike contraption to clear the floor before it could be opened. There was no way it could be forced from the outside. It was a protection, Karl had told her earlier, left over from the days when women were virgins and men were beasts.

"The good old days," Christa had sighed.

"You think women should still be virgins?" His eyebrows lifted in amusement.

"I was thinking more of men being beasts."

"You would like to be ravished?" he asked her, moving toward her menacingly, his eyes narrow slits.

She yawned, pretending indifference. "It might be nice for a change." Karl swept her up into his arms and dumped her on the bed, one hand going to the neckline of her blouse. "Don't rip it," she cried, laughing, grabbing hold of his arm and holding it still. He let go instantly. "No ripping, no ravishing." But he stayed to make love to her anyway.

Later she had watched him climb over the railing

of her balcony, descend some rough steps cut into the side wall of the castle and land on a walkway one floor below leading to his rooms. He had flourished a courtly bow to her, and she had thrown him a kiss.

"Dear God, how I've missed you," he broke into her thoughts, bringing her back to the present and the cold dimness. "I forget how to laugh when you're not here."

She looked around. "Where are we, anyway?"

"It's the wine cellar."

The room was a rough octagon, the walls broken at even intervals by arches protected by iron gates with modern-looking locks on them. Behind the bars she could barely make out wine bottles, piled tier on tier. There were six small barred alcoves opening off the main room. Under the flickering oil lamp were a long scarred wooden table and benches, and a cabinet filled with glasses was against one wall. A German phrase was carved over the arch facing the entrance, but Christa could not make it out. "What does that say?"

"Never empty," Karl translated for her. "It's written on all our labels."

"Appropriate for a wine cellar," Christa said.

"Originally it didn't refer to the wine. This used to be the dungeon, and it was quite literally never empty. Then when dungeons and private prisons became passé, some enterprising ancestor realized the room's potential as a wine cellar and gave the motto new meaning."

Christa walked slowly around, glancing into the locked cells that now took on less pleasant connotations. "How many bottles of wine do you have here?"

"I'm not sure. The exact number is upstairs in my office, if you'd really like to know."

"Some of them look pretty old."

"Some of them are. We have some bottles that go back maybe seventy years."

"What's it like to drink wine that was bottled before you were born?" she asked, turning to look at him.

"It's an emotional experience, painful in some ways. I would have said torturous, but then you would have felt obligated to advise me that this would be the place to feel tortured."

"Never! I never would have said that," she protested, "it's much too obvious. I can see where it would be difficult. You're drinking something irreplaceable."

"It's more than that. I think the history of this wine affects me more than most people. For me it's almost a communion. We'll decant one of the old bottles while you're here."

Christa faced Karl across the shadowy room, aware of the gift he was offering, "Thank you," she said simply.

"You're welcome. Now come on," he urged, his mood much improved. "I want to show you the vineyards."

He made a brief inspection to be sure everything was securely fastened, let her out and relocked the massive oak door after them.

"Are you afraid of thieves?"

"Not as long as the door is locked. A guard comes by frequently to check."

"Just one guard?" she asked as they climbed the stairs.

"Just one."

"Sort of a skeleton crew." He groaned at her humor.

They crossed a small cemented area at the back of the castle, passed through a gate in the wall and stood on the Bertastrasse, the street that ran under Christa's window. Some of the entrances to houses they passed were still damp from their daily morning scrubbing. Here and there niches had been carved into the stucco walls to hold small vases of flowers.

"Everything is so tenderly cared for," she said.

At the corner they turned right and the mountain loomed in front of them. Karl led her to a series of steps cut into the side of the hill and they began to climb. The dusky smell of grapes and cultivated earth was everywhere.

"How are you doing?" he asked halfway up.

"Fine," she lied, waving him on. She followed doggedly in his footsteps, refusing to think about the drop behind her. The sun, which had been pleasant, was becoming oppressive. Fortunately there was a breeze, and she felt the perspiration evaporate almost as quickly as it formed. The steps ended at a small structure, hardly more than a wooden roof supported by wooden beams. A rose-and-blue pennant fluttered from its peak and Christa could make out the same stylized lion on it that was carved into the pediment above the castle's main door. She stepped onto the flat earthen floor and breathed a sigh of relief, lifting her hair off her hot neck.

"It's a climb," Karl agreed, walking toward a long wooden bench at the back of the hut.

Christa sat down and surveyed the view. Karl remained standing, facing her. She gazed down the long slope of vineyards to the turreted castle and its grounds. From this distance they appeared precise and manicured. The stones of the castle glistened in the sun, while beyond it, outlined against the shining river, were the tiny shops of the Auguststrasse. To their right, at the end of the narrow gray line of the Bertastrasse, nestled the tiny church of St. Martin. Sounding as if it were coming from another country, the bell in the church tower began to toll. The air was heavy with early summer and the busyness of insects. Karl watched Christa's face intently.

She took a long time absorbing the view, then raised her eyes slowly to his. "It's beautiful."

He sat down next to her and took her hand. "This is my history. My ancestors accomplished all this."

Her hand lay still in his as they looked out at the shimmering village. All was peaceful. There were no airplanes, no automobile horns, no mechanical noises of any kind. There was only the restless movement of the vines ruffled by the breeze.

"Who built the castle?" Christa wanted to know.

"Most of the credit goes to Conrad Lothair. He was given this mountain because of his help in Barbarossa's wars against Denmark. Do you know anything about Barbarossa? If not, I'm not surprised—most people don't. It's amazing, though, how history means much more to you if you're living on it. Anyway, the German princes needed a place here along the Mosel, for bargemen to stop. River trade was a big part of their economy."

"So Conrad built the castle as a kind of inn?"

"A fortified inn, though it was never involved in much fighting. It's not in a strategic defensive position. That's why so much of it is still intact."

"It's been in your family ever since?"

"Almost. About the middle of the fourteenth century one of the von Klees had delusions of grandeur. He went on a building spree and added, along with a lot of other things, an immense banquet hall. They had jousting tournaments in the thing," he said, trying to impress its size on her. "He buried a wine vat under the hall and whenever he wanted wine he rang a bell, opened a spigot and the servants pumped it up to him."

"Indoor plumbing," Christa observed wonderingly.

"He died leaving the family bankrupt. They razed the additions and sold the stone and timbers to pay off some of the debt, but they couldn't clear all of it. Eventually the castle was taken over by a family of Frenchmen."

"And then what?"

"Legend has it that God came to our rescue. The French held the castle until a pestilence killed them. It killed half the German population too, but the von Klees, who survived, simply moved back in."

"And you've been here ever since."

"A thousand years, with the exception of that brief French occupation."

And if Karl had anything to do with it, they would be here a thousand more. His fingers tightened on her hand, and she knew he was waiting for her to say something.

Christa supposed she could lie and could say how impressed she was, but it was hardly something she could get excited about. Karl's life—unlike hers—was wine and ancestral history. But there was an ancient dignity about the place that pulled at her, and she could feel herself girding up to resist its appeal. She looked at their hands, their entwined fingers. Karl was holding hers so tightly her fingers were numb.

"It's magnificent," she said. He brought her hand to his lips and kissed it.

"Someday I would like it to belong to our children."

She didn't answer him. There was a great sadness in her that all the loveliness spread before her failed to erase.

8

CHRISTA RELAXED on the terrace that opened off the dining room. It was just after lunch, and the sun lay in bright wedges on the stones, dividing them into geometric shapes of light and dark. It was very pleasant sitting there, letting the sun warm her bones. Karl had left her on her own today; Wilhelm Tietjen, the wine broker, had finally arrived. But Christa had no complaints. Since her arrival, Karl had been almost her constant companion, and they had visited all the places of major interest in the immediate countryside. Once in a while he would pull himself away from her to take care of some urgent business, but most of the time they'd been together. Christa knew there were evenings when Karl worked well past midnight in order to spend most of the day with her. And since Edythe had stopped making references to the work piling up in the winery offices, he must have been keeping ahead of things.

Edythe was an education for Christa. She had never met anyone quite like her. She was never rude, always had time to talk, but there was a reserve to her that Christa could not get past. She finally decided that it was a cultural difference that had nothing to do with her personally since she detected that same reserve in Edythe's dealings with Karl. And, although she was warmer with Stephan, she seemed unable to give even her own son the easy kind of affection Christa had grown up with. Edythe reminded Christa of an emissary caught in a compromising position, not sure which side if any she should align herself with.

Christa had no such problems with Stephan. If anything, her problems with him were the reverse. He sought her out constantly, and she was always on guard when he was around, despite his charming manner. In fact, she sensed such a current of antagonism in his words, such a feeling that she was the pawn in a game he was playing with Karl, that spending time with him was exhausting. So it was with some dismay that she saw him approach now, a frosted stein held jauntily in his hand.

"May I join you?"

"All right," she said, watching him sit down at a small table alongside her chaise longue. He took a drink of his beer, then studied her over the rim of the stein so long she finally asked him what he was thinking about.

"I've been trying to decide for some days now just what the relationship is between you and Karl. Forgive me, but that question interests me. I have spent a good deal of time trying to decide just how much it encompasses. I mean, is it camaraderie? The kind that stands through thick and thin, sun and rain, wealth and poverty? Or is it more even than that?"

"We've been friends a long time," Christa said

cautiously, feeling she would have been wiser not to answer at all.

"What I really want to know is, are you lovers?"

She drew a deep shaky breath. "What possible business is that of yours?"

"In a long, roundabout way, it *is* my business. But I see by your face you're not about to satisfy my curiosity."

"You're very rude, Mr. Schröder," Christa asserted.

"Stephan," he corrected her, "and I know it. As patience is my virtue, rudeness is my vice. I apologize—I didn't mean to make you angry. I have nothing against you and Karl being lovers. I just wanted to know for sure. It would explain some of your reactions to me. Where are you going?" he asked as she swung her legs over the side of the chaise and stood up.

"I'm not enjoying our conversation, and I'm going to leave," she told him, her cheeks flushed.

"Don't do that," he protested, laughing. "I'll mind my manners. You think I'm a bastard, don't you—I can see it in your eyes. I suppose I have Karl to thank for that. Has he filled you with all sorts of information about me? None of it's true, you know. Karl and I are simply carrying out our assigned roles. He is the heir and I'm the black sheep. Together we keep the old ways going. Sit down." His voice had lost its teasing tone and had become insistent. "We'll talk about something pleasant. Tell me about yourself. I do know that you live in Boston and you're independent. I'm interested in the working class—for purely intellectual reasons, you understand. Though I hate to dwell on the thought, someday I might be forced to be one of them." He let his eyes slide deliberately over her body. "However, with you I could stretch my interest to include more than just intellect."

"It wouldn't be worth the effort," she warned, looking away. How she wished he'd go!

"You don't know that," Stephan said, grasping her wrist and gently tugging her down onto the chaise. He observed her for a moment, then shook his head. "Something tells me you're one of the new breed of women, self-sufficient and determined to make it on your own."

"That's true," Christa agreed, relieved to be off the subject of Karl.

"Such a waste, but it is a refreshing change from the women I'm used to dealing with. In the long run, it's probably a good thing. Were you wealthy, even marginally so, I'd feel a great urge to pursue you, and Karl would undoubtedly feel an equal urge to run me through. We shall have to content ourselves with friendship. Providing you can force yourself to stop thinking of me in Karl's terms." His face was in shadow and it was hard to tell if his eyes held a glint of amusement, if he were baiting her.

"Karl doesn't dictate anything to me."

"You mean in such a short time you have come to the conclusion all by yourself that I'm not worth liking? I find that difficult to believe." Stephan's pique was masked by his cool tone.

"Which part of that are you having trouble

with—my not liking you or the short amount of time it seems to have taken?" she challenged.

"Both actually. I'm not a bad type. I have rather a large collection of friends willing to attest to that."

"Good, then how I feel about you shouldn't matter at all."

"That's true." He took a long swallow of beer and placed the stein heavily on the table. "Except that it does. I don't like the idea that my cousin is blackening my name."

"Karl has said next to nothing about you. You've barely entered our conversation."

He went on as if he hadn't heard her. "I do not sully him, though, believe me, I have more cause to do so than he has. Has he told you that I am against him, that he is lonely and in need of comfort and that his father was maligned and put upon by the rest of us? I am not the bastard—" Stephan's voice was matter-of-fact, as if he were discussing the weather "—Karl is."

"I don't want to hear this."

"You'll stay there until I'm finished. I object to your deciding that I'm the enemy without having all the facts. I think there are some things you should know." He leaned forward so that the sun glittered in his eyes, keeping her prisoner as effectively as if he'd held her. "It's a fairy tale to go with our fairy-tale life here.

"Once upon a time, long, long ago, there lived a timid, susceptible man, who fell prey to a woman who had all the strengths he lacked. Using her feminine wiles she made it necessary for him to marry her." Stephan patted his stomach and studied Christa to be sure she understood what he meant. "It seemed to come as a shock to her that marriage did not change the timorous gentleman. Though nominally he controlled great wealth, actually he had control of nothing because he was nothing. She then set about punishing him for the sin of being exactly what he appeared to be. She insisted on flying home to America to have their baby, 'where doctors know what they are doing.' She stayed at a hospital in New York in a suite of rooms usually reserved for movie stars or heads of state. When she came back, a nurse was hired for the child so that his mother could travel and try to forget what a mistake she had married. She liked the name the marriage had given her, so long as she didn't have to put up with the man.

"She stayed at the finest hotels in Europe until the family put pressure on her husband to bring her home. By that time, the amount of money that spineless man had allowed her to spend was astronomical. She came back, but she threatened to leave him permanently and take his son with her if he didn't allow her to continue living as she had been. In searching for a way to cover what she had already spent and what she was threatening to spend in the future, he was drawn into a scheme."

Despite herself, Christa was fascinated by the repellent tale. "He agreed to supply an importing company in Australia with what appeared to be expensive French Burgundy," Stephan continued. "Unfortunately, only the label on the bottle was expensive. Its content was cheap table wine. By this clever manipulation the professor and the importer were able to sell a bottle of wine costing less than two dollars to produce, for more than fifty. The margin of profit was astounding. The next year they did the same thing. They thought they were safe, since the wine was supposed to age in the bottle for at least another ten years. By that time Karl's father hoped his connection with the fraud would have been long forgotten.

"But they failed to take into consideration the curiosity of Australians, who're almost as bad as Americans when it comes to that. Somebody, examining the bottle closely, probably trying to figure out what in the world made it worth fifty dollars, discovered that the French Burgundy had been glassed in a bottle bearing the imprint of a Spanish firm known for its inexpensive product. His suspicions aroused, he opened the bottle, sampled its contents and cried fraud. The importer was put out of business by the Australian authorities, and the good name of von Klee was tarnished almost beyond repair. The professor was forced to retire, and like a good, supportive wife, Lillian left him and took Karl with her to America. Nobody lived happily ever after."

Stephan observed the expression on Christa's face with satisfaction. "May I assume that my cousin has not yet found the opportunity to tell you this story?" When she still remained mute, he added, "You see, things are not always as black and white as they seem. Sometimes the good guys aren't all that good."

It was a tragic story, and Christa knew immediately that it was true. It explained the sadness that had surrounded the professor and the sometimes baffling relationship Karl had had with his father.

"If Lillian had not been so clever and my uncle so gullible, I would have been next in line, and I would not have to waste my energies ingratiating myself with people who can make it possible for me to live the way I want to." Stephan's words were bitter.

"You can't hold Karl responsible for the fact that he was born," Christa said, uncomfortable with the intensity in Stephan's voice. "Besides, Karl says you have no interest in the winery, that you prefer to live away. There's more than enough work here for two, if you were willing."

He laughed but the sound was wrong, off center somehow. "I thought you and Karl never discussed me? Besides, you've misread me completely if you think that I would ever be satisfied taking orders from him. He has no right to his position, he has no right to the winery. His father brought it to the brink of ruin, and it was my mother who saved it."

"How?" Christa asked in spite of herself, feeling even as she did that it was disloyal to Karl to be talking like this with Stephan.

"She persuaded Marcel Chenard to invest in us in the form of bonds, which gave us enough time to get back on our feet. For years things went along fairly well. Then Lillian died, Karl came back and the professor underwent a personality change. All of a sudden he was aggressive. He insisted that he be allowed to take control again. I guess he didn't want Karl to realize what a failure his father was. He was willing to go to court to be reinstated. The family decided that the name of von Klee couldn't stand up to another court case so they bargained with him. My mother would keep control until Karl came of age and then the winery would be turned over to him. You can see how that decision helped Karl and me to become the friends we are today."

"None of that is Karl's fault."

"Nor is it mine. It just is. But—" he held one finger up "—divine justice may yet be on my side. The Chenard bonds are due to mature in a few years, and if Karl can't buy them back they're automatically renewed for another twenty-five years, with the provision that Marcel Chenard takes command."

"But that would mark the end for all of you."

He smiled at her. "Use your head."

"Yvette," she said.

"She *is* Marcel's only child, and they both seem to like me." He examined his nails. "Though at the moment she's playing hard to get. I imagine she's waiting to see which way my financial winds will blow. I suppose I'd do the same if our positions were reversed."

"It wouldn't bother you that the winery wouldn't be under von Klee control any more?"

"After a thousand years, maybe it's time for a change." He leaned back and decided to change the subject. "You know, this is interesting. In all the time the winery has been under the von Klees, there has never been a generation that did not produce a son of a first son. I trust Karl investigated your background to see that there is a solid history of uncomplicated pregnancies?" He turned to look at her, his eyes sharp and level. "Nothing means more to him than the winery. If he loses it you can count yourself lucky. Besides, you would probably not be happy living here. You're too American."

Christa knew that deep inside she felt he was right. She remained silent.

"It shows up in ways fascinating to observe," he went on. "The way you put me in my place, for example, and the way you react to my mother. You're never rude but your attitude says, 'I'm just as important in my way as you are.' It's refreshing, but it would make life difficult for you here."

"You see yourself then, as the rightful person to be in charge?"

"Your tone of voice tells me you don't think much of that idea. But I won't take it to heart. After all, you are working on the basis of a decision made about me before you had all the facts. My cousin was remiss in not giving them to you, because you cannot form an educated opinion without them. Karl's emotionalism has colored your thinking in many ways. There is nothing to running a winery. As businesses go this one is fairly simple—pick, crush, bottle, sell and take off for Cannes until the next harvest.

"Has all this upset you?" His tone was solicitous but his eyes held no softness. He put the stein down heavily on the table and folded his hands in his lap, considering her. She let the silence drag on. "We seem to have run out of conversation," he observed. "I had toyed with the idea of inviting you to go with me to Trier to see the Roman ruins, but it doesn't seem like such a good idea anymore." He lifted himself out of the chair and stretched, then checked his watch. "Karl and our wine broker have been at it now for several hours. Maybe I'll wander past the offices and see what stage negotiations have reached."

"What will you do if Karl stays in control?" Christa asked anxiously.

"Wait until next year," he replied, walking away from her, his hands sunk in the pockets of his pants.

Christa released a long sigh. She was weighted down with information that, given the choice, she would prefer not to have received, at least not from Stephan.

Leaving the terrace, she passed through the empty dining room and quiet reception area and climbed the stairs to Marietta's rooms, pausing in front of the mirrored door on the armoire. *You're very American*, Stephan had said. She examined herself and tried to see it. She wondered how American Karl's mother had been. She wondered if she had trapped Karl's father or been trapped by circumstances. What would it be like to live here? Einzell was different from any other place Christa had been. It had a rhythm all its own and almost seemed to exist in its own time zone. Not far away, in the cities, life was reminiscent of Boston, a Boston that had been scrubbed clean and left shining: immaculate shopping malls, symphony halls, movie houses and crowds of fast-moving, sophisticated people. Karl had taken Christa to Frankfurt and Mainz and she had loved both of them, but she had always been aware that Einzell awaited them.

During the day when the young people were at work, the village was inhabited by old women wearing housedresses, black cardigans and flowered kerchiefs tied around their heads. Once Christa had been sitting by the river watching two village women approach each other from opposite directions. They had stopped to talk and then continued on. Christa had smiled to herself. It had been like watching someone walk through a mirror. She had told Karl her observations and he had laughed. "That's the old Germany," he had told her. "Someday it will be gone completely, and something wonderful will have been lost."

The younger women, however, whom she had seen in the bakery and on walks along the river in the evening were almost as contemporary as women in the States. What a land of contrasts!

Christa left the mirror and walked rapidly across the room and out onto her narrow terrace. Einzell lay before her, seductively peaceful, the vineyards behind it, the streets resting in shadows, the inhabitants safe behind doors that closed on simple lives. Why hadn't Karl told her his story, told her why he was so desperate to raise money? The fact that he had withheld the information gave her a feeling of uneasiness, reinforcing a thought she'd had once before. There was a Karl she didn't know. What was she doing here, enmeshed in a family argument that had all the overtones of operatic tragedy? "He'll never leave this place," she said aloud—she was foolish if she thought otherwise. There was only one decision to be made and it was hers. Could she live here with him? The possibility of his leaving Germany to live in Boston was nonexistent. As always, she put the question out of her mind. There would be time enough later to think it through.

She wandered back into the bedroom and stretched out on the bed, wondering herself how things were going between Karl and Wilhelm. Besides his plans for advertising she knew Karl was suggesting to the small local growers that they form their own cooperative and market the wine under the von Klee label. Their agreement was crucial to the winery's success. She opened a novel and tried to lose herself in it, but finally closed it and stared unseeing at the foot of her bed. All that bitterness, and Karl had chosen not to share any of it with her. She lay there, trying not to think what it all meant, until the bells of St. Martin's sounded their evening alarm. Dinner would be served in one hour and still no word from Karl.

Christa showered and purposely dressed in a bright yellow silk skirt and blouse, the short sleeves loose and full, the neckline falling in a soft vee. But neither the shower nor the bright colors did anything to wash away the heavy residue of the afternoon.

Before she reached the bottom of the staircase she could hear voices. They seemed to be talking animatedly and with humor, judging by the frequent laughter that punctuated the conversation. She pulled open the door to the reception area to find Karl, Wilhelm Tietjen and three other men she had not seen before standing in a relaxed group, wineglasses in their hands, enjoying one another's company.

Karl turned as the door opened, and seeing Christa he smiled broadly and came toward her. Her heart swelled with love and, gripping his hand, she followed him back to the group. He squeezed her hand briefly before he left to get her some wine, and Christa made polite small talk with the men until he came back with her drink.

"Karl tells us you've had quite a bit of experience with advertising," Fabiani, one of the men, commented. "He said a lot of other things, too, and we accused him of exaggerating. Now that I've met you, I can see that he wasn't." Christa grinned at his pleasantries. He drained his wine, handed Karl his glass and said, "It's time to go. We'll see you tonight?" He turned to Christa. "I look forward to talking to you." There was a low whistle from one of the other men. "About business," Fabiani said, "strictly business."

There was some appreciative laughter and Karl walked with the men to the door. Wilhelm placed his empty glass on one of the small tables and turned to Karl. He grasped him by both shoulders and gave him a friendly shake, then patted him smartly on the back. "If you'll excuse me, now," Wilhelm said to Christa, "I'd like to wash up before dinner."

Karl waited a moment to be sure Wilhelm was gone, then he grabbed her in a bear hug, lifting her off her feet so that she was looking down at him. His exuberance was contagious, and she had to smile. "I take it things went well," she said, resting her hands on his shoulders.

"Very well, very, very well. Not only is Wilhelm enthusiastic about the advertising campaign, but the men who were here are some of the small growers in the area. They've agreed to come in with me—to leave the cooperative they've been dealing with in Mainz and join one with us. It will triple the amount of wine we can sell, because eventually I think all the small growers around here will join us. It's going to work," he whispered softly, staring up at her. "You've brought me luck." He lowered her slowly, sliding her body along his until he was able to reach her lips.

Footsteps sounded on the circular stairs and Karl set her quickly down. She took one step away from him as the stairway door opened. Stephan looked at their flushed faces and drew his own conclusions as to what had gone on. "It hasn't been settled yet," he said quietly, walking past them into the dining room.

"What does he mean?" Christa asked Karl tensely.

Karl ran his hands through his hair and sighed. "It's not something I can explain in a few words, and right now I don't even want to think about it. Tonight I want to be happy." He held her lightly by the elbow, guiding her toward the dining room.

Dinner was a tangled affair, where what was said was not necessarily what was meant. Karl was in good spirits and tried to keep things going, but for the most part the conversation was desultory. Even Christa didn't seem able to supply the interesting small talk that oiled the wheels of conversation. Wilhelm joined them, and during one of the frequent pauses in the flow of talk he made a comment about Fabiani's joining them. Stephan gave him a long measured look, then said to Karl, "You get several points on that score, cousin. I never believed they would do it."

"They produce a very common wine," Edythe said, as if she were not sure this new development was to her liking. "In no way can it compare with ours."

"It can be improved," Karl told her. "If someone who is knowledgeable takes over the decision-making, quality will go up. They ruined a ton of grapes last year because someone insisted on adding sugar. Those particular grapes should have been left alone, allowed to run off their skins naturally instead of being pressed the way they were. They could have ended up with a decent, light wine."

"The expert is back with us again." Stephan's voice had lost any playfulness it had held over the past few days and was openly hostile. "Last year he spent almost forty-eight hours agonizing over what kind of yeast to begin the fermentation process with. You take that long to make decisions and all the advertising in the world won't help you."

"Karl is an excellent wine master." Wilhelm's

tone was gentle but firm. "In my years as a broker I have met only a few men whose instincts are nearly always right, and Karl is one of them. I think the cooperative will do very well." Christa thought of Stephan's comment—pick, crush, bottle, sell and take off for Cannes until the next harvest. "These old wineries," Wilhelm continued gently, "are treasures. They should be kept going as long as possible."

Stephan looked from Wilhelm to Karl and then pushed his chair back roughly from the table. "I seem to have lost my appetite. If you'll excuse me?"

The conversation turned away from present business and Christa lost track of it. She was noticing how relaxed Karl was, how even the skirmish with Stephan hadn't seemed to upset him. When she refused the apple kuchen that was being served for dessert, Karl folded his napkin and stood up. "If you'll excuse us, Miss Monroe and I are going to Frau Mahler's to celebrate."

"Ah," Wilhelm said, a pleased smile on his face, "Christa should enjoy that."

Christa smiled a good-night to everyone, and Edythe smiled back, her expression an attempt at lightness, her troubled eyes spoiling the effect.

9

THE PORSCHE HUMMED purposefully along the Auguststrasse, and Karl sat relaxed at the wheel, his profile outlined against the still, light river. Every once in a while he turned to smile at Christa.

"Karl, how will a cooperative help? I know you'll have more wine to sell, but the profits will have to be shared by a lot more people." Christa leaned toward Karl, eager for his answer.

"We'll get a percentage of all the wine sold because the processing will be done in our sheds and I'll be in control. On top of that we'll handle the business end of things, including our successful advertising campaign, and we'll receive money for that also. It may not amount to a great deal the first year, but as more and more growers come in with us, it will be enough."

Christa put her hand in his, and Karl turned up her palm and kissed it gently. "Do you realize that with the exception of mealtimes I haven't seen you at all today?" he said. She did realize it.

"That's much too long," Karl went on. "I'll have to see that it doesn't happen again." It had gotten dark enough that he needed the headlights, and he bent forward to switch them on. "What did you do while I was involved with Wilhelm?"

"Not much. I read and generally just lazed about. I talked to Stephan for a while." He looked at her sharply, but she refused to meet his look. They would eventually discuss what Stephan had told her, but not now. "Where are we going tonight?" she asked, changing the subject.

"Frau Mahler's." He grinned. "It's a *Weinstube*, an English-type pub without the inhibitions."

She rested her head against the seat and watched the dim scenery pass. Karl's hand was warm in hers, and she looked down at them, one slim and freckled, the other dark and strong. If his mother hadn't died maybe he would have grown up in New England, and they might have met there—both of them with roots firmly planted on the same side of the Atlantic.

They pulled into a cobbled courtyard behind an ancient building, and he led her down a flight of stone steps and into a cellar. Frau Mahler herself greeted them, calling Karl by name. "Such a long time," she scolded, her hands on her hips, generous mouth stretched in a smile. She was totally overdone, from the rustling black taffeta of her low-cut evening gown to the immense false lashes that ringed her heavily made-up eyes. But her smile was sincere. "Tonight will be good," she said, "Jocko is coming. You can find your own table, *ja*?" She smiled at Christa.

"*Ja*," Christa answered, charmed by the woman. Frau Mahler clapped her on the back and sent them on their way. They stepped down into a white stucco room with rough exposed beams and timbered walls. A deep shelf ran around the walls two feet below the ceiling. On the shelf were stuffed birds, small game animals, large bottles, old pottery, all of it covered with dust and looking as if it hadn't been touched in years. It was the first dust she'd seen since leaving Boston, and it almost made her homesick. Karl noticed her eyeing the clutter. "They're all gifts from patrons, and every item has a story. Next time we come I'll begin to tell you about them. Tonight you'll have enough to absorb."

As they moved into the room she saw that there were mannequins in every corner, dressed in outlandish clothes. The female dummies had jewelry of every description draped or pinned all over them; the "men" wore an assortment of hats, vests and scarves. As she watched, a couple came in and paused, while the girl carefully removed a long bead necklace and charm bracelet from a dummy's arm and put them on. The man pulled a garish purple and yellow scarf from around a male model's neck and stuffed it in his shirt pocket so that it puffed out like a flower. Then he grabbed a Greek fisherman's cap from the stack on the model's head and placed it on his own.

Karl steered Christa toward a long wooden table that already held a group of people. As they approached, one of the men looked up and got to his feet instantly, his arms wide open in welcome. It was Fabiani. Then a boy plunked steins of dark beer down on the table, even at places where as yet no one was sitting.

"Good," a voice said behind her. "I see we have arrived just in the nick of time." She turned to see the man wearing the Greek fisherman's cap.

Karl introduced Christa to the newcomer, whose name was Paul. Fabiani reached under the table and took out an old Prussian helmet. He placed it on his head before shaking hands with Paul, who laughed and said, "So you wear the helmet tonight."

"It's probably my death warrant," Fabiani said. A sweet-faced blond woman sitting next to him looked at Christa and rolled her eyes as if to say, "They never grow up, do they?" She moved over and Christa slid onto the bench next to her.

"All right, what are the rest of you wearing?" Hats were pulled out and placed at varying angles on various heads. "And you?" Fabiani looked at Karl.

"Nothing tonight."

A wave of disappointment went around the table. "You know how it slows things down when someone is sober."

"I can't help it," Karl said, laughing. "I have to be clear-headed in the morning."

"So do we all."

"No," Fabiani said. "Karl is right. He has some important work to do tomorrow, and since my future is now closely involved with his, I'd just as soon he watch himself. By the way—" he turned to Paul "—where do you stand?"

"I told you I wasn't sure," Paul said. "I'm watching. If it works I'm with you. We just can't take any chances right now." He patted his wife's slightly rounded stomach. "Well," he said, ceremoniously adjusting his cuffs, "shall we begin?" He raised his stein and nodded toward Fabiani.

"It's the beginning of the end," Fabiani mourned. He perched the helmet on his head and the two of them downed their beer, wiping the foam from their mouths with the backs of their hands. Paul bowed his thanks, removed the cap and sat down. All night long hats were put on and taken off, and every time someone wearing a hat challenged Fabiani, he had to don the helmet and match the challenger drink for drink until he felt that he had reached his limit. Then the helmet was given to someone else. An exact accounting of the time it took before each person gave up the helmet was kept, and at the end of the evening the man who had worn it longest had his bill taken care of by the others.

As the evening wore on, Christa's German improved. At least she thought it did. She seemed able to say things she didn't realize she knew the words for—although judging from the laughter that accompanied much of what she said, maybe she still didn't have the words. But the laughter was warm and welcoming, and she felt totally at ease.

She sat next to Fabiani's wife Elena, across from the pregnant Marta. "When is the baby due?" Christa asked her.

"November," the young woman replied.

"A good wife," Elena observed. "She'll wait until after the grapes have been picked."

Marta laughed. "I wish it had been as well-thought-out as that. We have another little boy," she said, stressing the word *little*, "and I was hoping to wait a bit before giving him a brother."

"A brother," Elena commented with a grimace.

"You know men," Marta said, smiling.

"Do you have any children?" Christa asked Elena.

"Not yet," she replied. "I'm too busy!"

"Elena works for a designer," Marta explained, giving the name of a man whose dresses were often seen in the pages of fashion magazines.

"Really? I've heard of his work," and Christa went on to tell them about her association with Lass Rollan. They got into a spirited discussion about fashion and various lines. Elena was fascinated with what Christa had been doing and suggested that, if she was going to be in Germany long enough, she stop in and talk to her employer.

"My closest connection with fashion these days is trying to decide which shirt Willie should wear for his outing." Marta sighed.

"Don't give me that nonsense," Elena retorted with a grin. "You know you're crazy about that child."

Marta grinned in agreement. "That doesn't stop me from wanting to know what's going on in the rest of the world."

"All right, if Christa can find the time to meet with Helmut, you come, too. And after the business talk is over, we'll go have lunch someplace elegant. Okay?" Elena looked at Christa, who smiled and nodded, then at Marta, who made the classic sign of agreement, her thumb and index finger joined in a circle.

Then Jocko arrived, a short, stocky man so weathered that his age was hard to determine.

Dressed in corduroy pants and bright red suspenders, with an accordion strapped to his back, he received an enthusiastic ovation from the crowd. He passed from table to table playing popular music and Christa could hear the clink of coins being dropped into his cup.

"Is there enough?" someone shouted when he stopped to count them. He shook his head and toured the tables again. "Now?" the crowd asked as he stopped once more to count. He cocked his head and smiled, raising his shoulders and placing his hands palms up. There was a collective groan. "How much more?" He held both hands up, fingers outstretched. Men dug into their pockets, and money was stuffed into the cup until Jocko called a halt. Dumping what he had collected into a worn leather pouch, Jocko tied it carefully onto his belt and took up his position in the center of the room. Frau Mahler stood at the room's entrance, smiling happily, tables were pushed out of the way and, stamping his feet three times loudly on the floor, Jocko pounded out old German dancing songs.

Everyone danced until they were exhausted and sang until they were hoarse. Much too soon, Karl said he and Christa had to leave.

"My friend," Paul complained, "we hardly see you, and now you're leaving already."

"We'll get together again soon," Karl said, his arm around Christa's shoulder.

"We will, too," Elena said. "How long will you be in Germany, Christa?"

Such a simple question with so many complications in its answer. Had everyone really stopped talking to hear what Christa said, or did it only seem that way? "I'm afraid my time this trip is going by too fast," she hedged.

"Well, if you find you have time on your hands, if Karl will let you out of his sight, call me. Even if you haven't time to do any business, I'd like to have lunch with you."

She promised she would, said good-night to everyone and they made their way through the crowded room and out into the night. "You're walking funny," Karl remarked when they got outside.

"I'm fine," Christa said with a giggle, "just the slightest bit woozy, but fine."

He put his arm around her for support and they walked toward the car, bumping against each other. He stopped her halfway there and planted a kiss on her lips. All night, even when he was talking with the men, he'd been touching her—his hand on her shoulder, his leg pressed against hers. "That was fun," he said, smiling down at her.

"How do you know those people?"

"Some of them I grew up with, some of them I went to school with, some of them have worked at the vineyard."

"Hometown boys," Christa said. "They think a lot of you."

Karl unlocked the car door and she got in. He slid behind the wheel and backed out onto the road. It stretched before them so clearly in the moonlight that he didn't turn on the headlights. "When I was growing up," Karl said with an old bitterness, "those hometown boys had some names for me that were not very flattering."

"They respect you now."

"Yes." There was satisfaction in his voice. "But only because I've earned it."

His expression was masked by shadows, and though his voice was firm and his words confident, she felt his vulnerability. "Why didn't you tell me about your father?"

He was silent so long she was afraid he was not going to answer her. "I see Stephan made good use of his time."

"Is it true?" she persisted, hoping it wasn't.

"Yes, though I'm sure Stephan embellished it somewhat."

"He said your mother drove him to it."

"How nice that he was able to tell you everything."

"Why didn't *you* tell me? I'd have told you if it had been the other way around."

"Don't be too sure. You've never been ashamed of your parents. You have no idea what you'd do if you were."

"I'd have told you," she insisted. "It would have hurt too much not to."

"In that way, then, we're very different. We talked about self-esteem once, remember? I'm just now beginning to get mine back. Maybe when I've had it for a while I'll be able to talk about those things. But it will never be easy. I've lost the American ability to bare my soul and then discuss the weather as if nothing had happened."

She placed her hand lightly on his arm. "I don't want there to be any secrets between us Karl, ever."

"This wasn't a secret between us. It has nothing to do with you and me. I would have told you eventually, the time just never seemed to be right."

She leaned back in her seat and watched the silvered landscape pass. "He was a lovely man," she said. "Nothing will change my opinion on that score. He was weak and he made mistakes, but he obviously made them out of love. And he did love you, Karl, so please don't hold his faults against him."

He stared steadily ahead and then reached for her hand, bringing it to his lips. "I'm trying," he said. "Each day it gets easier, and I have you to thank for that. As a matter of fact, it scares me to think how many things are right in my life these days. So let's not talk of the past tonight; the present is much too precious." He cleared his throat and began to sing softly. Christa joined in, willing to let the subject drop. There would be another, better time to discuss it. The volume increased until they were singing at the top of their lungs.

"That was awful," she said with a laugh when they were finished.

"You don't like my voice?" He pretended to be shocked.

"Don't feel badly, not everyone can sing. You dance very well though. I like the feel of your body next to mine."

"Is that the way proper young Bostonians talk?"

"I can't help it, I do. Your body is so different

from mine. I love the way your strong neck flows into your shoulders, and I love the swells and curves of your muscles. I even like the rough hair on your chest and the lean hardness of your legs."

He laughed softly. "Do you know what it's like to make love to you? Do you have any idea what it does to me when I touch you and you respond?"

"No," she teased, "tell me."

"Keep looking at me like that and I'll pull off the road and *show* you."

"That will never do," she said. "I'll stop looking at you." Like an obedient child, she closed her eyes. "Oh! With my eyes closed I'm awfully dizzy."

"Lucky one of us knows what he's doing."

"Both of us know what we're doing," she said in a drowsy voice. "It's just that one of us will remember it better tomorrow."

"That's too bad. Tonight shows every indication of being a memorable evening. Besides," he said, laughing, "you didn't have that much to drink."

"It doesn't take much," she said ruefully.

They were back in the sleeping town, passing the dark stores and the deserted intersection that led to St. Martin's. Karl turned through the old stone walls, passed the footings of a long-ago ruined gatehouse and drove down the rutted lane that led to the castle. The lawns and flower beds looked eerie in the moonlight. He shut off the engine, and the castle contemplated them.

"I think it tolerates me," Christa said, her head cocked to one side as she looked back at it, "but just barely."

"Come on, young lady, you've had a busy day." Karl held open the passenger door, but she remained inside staring at the castle. "It hasn't accepted me. It hasn't decided if I'll fit in."

Karl reached in and took her hand to pull her out. "I've noticed in the past that a night at a *Weinstube* often leads to this kind of conversation, but it's too late to get philosophical." He guided her under the stone entrance arch and through the oak front door, ten inches thick. In the hushed reception area one small light burned, its reflection diffused in the polished stones of the floor, their luster the result of generations of busy feet.

Christa's eyes were drawn to the framed faces that surrounded her. In the tender light the portrait of a young woman glowed, her ample shoulders bare, her upper arms and chest swathed in blue silk. "Who's that?"

"Maria Theresa, my great-great-aunt." Karl came up behind her and put his arms around her, burying his face in her hair.

"And that?" She pointed to the doleful-looking man in the painting beside her.

"Her husband."

"Poor thing. Are you going to end up looking like that?"

His answer was to kiss her lightly on the neck. She moved through the reception room, portrait by portrait, and Karl named and cataloged his ancestors. She stayed a long time in front of the portraits of two young girls painted on wood. The wood was deteriorating, but the faces still held a touching sweetness.

"They were twins," Karl said. "They died in the pestilence and it's said they haunt the garden. They were buried in unhallowed ground because there wasn't any room left in the churchyard."

"This place is not gentle with its women, is it?"

They had progressed to a great tapestry that hung nearly from the ceiling to the floor. Christa could pick out men on horseback and ladies sitting under trees in the vibrantly colored stitches. Across one side a stag leaped. Behind him, arrows at the ready, three hunters stood tensely in their saddles. "Thirteenth century," Karl said.

Christa drew in her breath. "The colors are so clear."

He turned her gently and led her to the spiral staircase. "When the French occupied the castle, they took that tapestry showing the hunting prowess of the von Klees and hung it in the stable between the stalls. It was a show of contempt. After the plague, when the family came back, they rescued it and rehung it in the hall." He held the door to the tower open for her and they started slowly up the stairs.

"Through the years, people commented on how the tapestry never faded, how brilliant the colors were. The von Klees, of course, again took that as a sign of divine favor. But science, being basically unromantic, shattered that theory. The examiners from the national museum think the ammonia fumes in the stable acted on the colors as a preservative. So the French inadvertently saved the thing they'd been trying to destroy."

"Is that true?"

"Every word."

They had reached Christa's floor and were walking along the corridor. "Karl, that tapestry and those portraits must be worth a fortune. Couldn't you sell them if you need to raise money?"

"No," he replied. "They belong to the estate. Besides, no one wants the portraits. The frames, maybe, but the paintings are worthless to anyone but us, and the tapestry isn't ours anymore. My grandfather willed it to the national museum, which will claim it when and if we break up housekeeping."

They reached the doorway to her room and she made a great show of looking up and down the hall, then whispered, "Can you come in?"

"I think I'd better," he whispered back. "I'm in no condition to climb the wall."

"My reputation is ruined anyway. Stephan knows about us."

"Stephan has a sixth sense about these things."

She closed the door quietly behind him. "Do you think Edythe can hear us?" she asked, a twinkle in her eye.

"The floors are two feet thick," he assured her, still whispering. "How much noise do you intend to make?"

"That depends." She narrowed her eyes, teasing.

He looked at her speculatively and then threw himself down in her small boudoir chair, his legs stretched out in front of him. "Turn down the bed, woman."

"Yes, sire," she whispered, and taking small hurried steps removed the chintz spread and folded it carefully on the chest. Then she turned back the corners of the down comforter and plumped the two down pillows, thumping an indentation precisely in the middle of each one. "For your royal head," she explained. He nodded in regal acceptance.

She knelt in front of him and untied his shoes, slipping his socks off and placing them beneath the bed. He regarded her impassively, though she could see a small smile lifting the corners of his lips. She tried to decide what should come next, and settled on his shirt.

"You're not cooperating," she complained in a singsong voice, as she tried to sit on his lap and failed because of the incline of his legs. Still silent, he raised his knees to give her something to perch on. She unbuttoned his shirt and loosened it from his pants, running her hands over the solid expanse of his chest and dropping a kiss on his mouth. His skin was cool, and she felt her way around to his back, while her tongue tentatively explored his lips. It filled her with joy to touch him like this, and she almost lost herself in sensual pleasure. But feeling his muscles tighten in response she drew back quickly, dancing away out of his reach, smiling a self-satisfied smile.

Watching him, she began to hum softly—harem-dancing music. Stretching, she ran her fingers through her hair to let it fall shimmering down her back. She stepped out of her sandals and swayed around the room, relishing the feel of his eyes on her, holding herself back from laughing out loud. With her back to him, she loosened the waistband of her skirt and let it sigh to the floor while she continued her slow weaving dance. She knew she was pleasing him and it lent energy to what she was doing. It also began a slow beat of desire in her. She came close to him and bent so that her hair brushed over his hands. He groaned softly and what she saw in his eyes made her pause, but shaking her finger at what she'd read there, she smiled lazily and backed away from him. Still humming, she shrugged out of her silk blouse, and in her slip tried unsuccessfully to imitate the rolling contortions of a belly dancer.

Karl laughed, a deep delicious sound, and Christa made a face at him, returning to her earlier, simpler movements. Gracefully she removed the rest of her clothes, timing it so that her satin bra dropped from the end of an outstretched finger as she hummed the final note of her performance. Then she stood by the bed naked, suddenly unsure of what to do next.

He was still slouched in the chair, his elbows resting on the wooden arms, his hands folded, his index fingers pressed against his lips. He was the picture of relaxed disinterest—except for his eyes smoldering under his brows and the throbbing beat of a vein in his temple. When he moved it was quickly. He pulled her to him, lifting her off her feet and driving the air from her lungs so that she had to push him away and gasp for breath.

"Look at you—" his voice was a hoarse whisper "—you're beautiful." His hands spread along her back, warming her skin where they touched her. She reached up to trace the shape of his head and as he buried his face in her hair, she heard him laughing.

"What is it?" She twisted her head to look at him.

"Where did you learn to dance like that?"

"Girl Scout camp?"

"I doubt it. You're a brazen hussy."

"Would you believe—" she paused between each word to kiss him "—there are men in Boston who swear I'm frigid?"

"Oh, God!" He laughed again. "What fools must live in Boston." His lips closed over hers, his tongue probed the softness of her mouth and she felt his arousal.

"Take your clothes off," she whispered.

"Is there no end to your shamelessness?"

"No," she said, working at his belt.

They lay sideways across the bed, the down quilt puffed around them, and Karl's mouth took its leisurely tour of her body, stopping here and there where he knew he could bring her pleasure. "You are the most extraordinary thing that's ever happened to me. You're never out of my mind—it's as if I'm obsessed."

Finally, she gave herself up to the emotions that sparkled inside her. There was passion and desire, but above all was a shining layer of happiness at just being here with him. She held him as close as was possible and the hard, masculine smell of him made her blood race. "I'm floating, Karl. I'm up there on the ceiling, a weightless, boneless package of bliss," and she tightened her hold even more as if to anchor herself.

"I wish I could tell you that I've never had anyone else," he said softly. "I wish you could have been the only one I'd shared this kind of closeness with. But you're the only one who has ever made me feel this way, who's ever meant this much to me."

"Hush," she said. "It doesn't matter. All that's important is right now. I want you to touch me, yes, like that," she sighed.

His nostrils flared and his mouth parted in that expression she remembered well. He wanted to possess her and she ached with the need to surrender. "Christa." His voice broke on her name and his eyes darkened. "I love you."

She stilled his confession with her mouth, and then she kissed his neck, his shoulders, his chest. She followed the trail of rough gold hair down the length of his body until it joined the short curling ruff between his legs.

With shaking hands he raised her head, and when she was lying alongside him he straddled her, never taking his eyes from hers. He moved against her, slowly, tantalizingly, teasing her the way she had teased him. She could barely raise her eyelids to look at him. "Do you want me?" His voice was a rasping whisper.

"Yes," she answered. "Oh, yes. Now!" she begged.

"Not yet." He touched her breasts, sculpting them with his mouth until her nipples rose in hard peaks, while his hands found her center and she writhed on the bed in an agony of desire. His mouth replaced his hand and with deliberate patience he increased the rhythm of his caresses until she tangled her hands in his hair and cried out.

"Please, Karl, please!"

No longer able to wait, he covered her body with his and entered her, and for one luminous moment they hung suspended, eyes locked, before they were lost in the radiance of fulfillment.

Afterward, she lay in his arms totally content, without the strength or desire to move. His lips lightly touched her face and brushed back the hair from her forehead. "You're my talisman," he said softly, "my protection against the world. Nothing can overcome what we have together, nothing can hurt me. And I won't let the world lay a finger on you."

"The world doesn't have fingers," she said softly. "Slings and arrows maybe, an insidious, twisted sense of humor possibly, but not fingers."

"The world does not have a sense of humor. I've always found it to be rather grim, until you came along."

"Yes, it does," she insisted. "Look what it's done to us."

"I like what it's done to us," he said with satisfaction.

"You would."

"And you don't?" He was suddenly wary.

"I can't talk about this now." Her voice was thick. "I'm drunk on love and happiness and anything I say should be ignored."

But he was not to be put off that easily. "Do you love me?"

She nodded.

"Say it," he demanded.

"I love you, Karl." She thought her heart would burst with joy at any moment.

"All right." He pulled the edges of the comforter around them and gathered her into his arms. "The rest isn't very important."

"Yes, it is," Christa replied, sadness suddenly gripping her. But she barely mouthed the words and Karl didn't hear them.

10

SHE WOKE WITH THE MEMORY of Karl's body still printed on hers. His place beside her was empty, but he had left a residue of memories. There was her bra, lying where she'd dropped it. Grinning at the memory of her performance, she hugged her pillow and debated skipping breakfast. She could stay here all morning and go over and over their lovemaking of last night, but the idea, while tempting, was also impractical.

Christa swam up through the bedclothes to a sitting position and contemplated the day ahead. There would be another meeting this morning in the winery offices one floor below, when Karl would show Wilhelm and the growers his carefully assembled facts and figures—how much business Fabiani and the others would bring in, and how much of the wine would be processed by hand rather than machine. That special wine would be bottled under a new label, destined for discriminating markets, heralded by an advertising campaign that would inform buyers of the uniqueness of the product. Hopefully, the ads would make the astronomical price of the wine palatable. "Our grapes lead a hand-to-mouth existence," was the slogan Christa had come up with to describe the new product. Karl hadn't known whether to groan or laugh. He still vacillated between thinking it was very good or very bad.

Karl would be busy all day again. She should go down to breakfast—after all, it might be the only time she would see him. He had warned her that once these meetings started his free time would be scarce. In other words, his vacation was over. Meanwhile Christa had received a letter from Katie saying all was well on the home front; the few calls that had come in, she had handled. Vera Eason had left word that Christa was to get in touch as soon as she got back. The letter had been both reassuring and upsetting. Of course there had been few calls. Without Christa there to drum up new business, there would be. She wondered how much time she had before she lost so much momentum in the competitive business community of Boston that she wouldn't be able to recoup.

Well, if she wasn't going to be busy with anything important, how should she spend her day? A feeling of displacement snaked some tendrils around her; everyone had something to do but her. "I'll take the car," she told herself. "Karl said I was free to use it and do some touring." That decided, she climbed out of bed.

"*Guten Tag, Fräulein Monroe,*" Edythe greeted her, looking up from her breakfast and smiling. Christa debated asking her to use her first name again, then decided not to. She suspected that Edythe was not comfortable calling her Christa.

There was an edge of formality to most encounters in Einzell, with the exception of last night at the *Weinstube*.

Christa was aware that this morning there was only the two of them. "Where is everybody?" she asked, returning Edythe's smile.

"Karl is in the offices with Wilhelm."

"And Stephan?"

Edythe gave her a quick look, as if trying to decide if the question were merely polite or if it indicated something more. "He's probably still asleep. He keeps erratic hours." Christa poured herself some coffee from the silver service on the table and sat down. Edythe rang the small china bell that sat next to her plate, and almost immediately the young girl who helped in the kitchen was there, asking Christa what she wanted this morning. Edythe waited until she was gone, then said, "Did you enjoy Frau Mahler's?"

"It was quite an experience," Christa replied cautiously.

"I haven't been there in a long time, but I think your assessment is right."

Christa's eyes roamed over the wood-paneled dining room, bright with morning sun. The doors to the terrace were wide open and a few lazy flies had joined them. No one seemed to care. Back in Leicester the meal would have come to a halt while the buzzing intruders were tracked down and flattened. Then the doors would have been closed until suitable screens had been fitted.

There were no screens on any of the windows in

the castle, but Christa was seldom bothered by insects in her room. "You're too high up," Karl told her. "German insects are only licensed to fly at forty feet." He was often very funny—she smiled to herself—but not with his family. With them he was someone else. Which Karl would win out if she stayed? Would the family have to adjust to *her* Karl, or would she have to adjust to theirs? She could not imagine their Karl having joined her in that bit of nonsense they had indulged in last night. She grinned again at the memory.

"It must be a very pleasant thought to have occupied you so completely."

She looked up to find Edythe smiling at her, and the rush of heat to her cheeks told Christa she was blushing. She searched her mind quickly for something to say, and asked a question she had been wondering about. "How many rooms are there here?"

"I think about forty. We've made some changes, taken down a few walls, so I'm not really sure. Most of them aren't used, but that figure is about right."

"Has anyone ever considered turning it back into an inn? Karl told me that's what it was to begin with."

"I know the idea has occurred to him. It's on his list of possibilities if the course he's outlined for the coming year doesn't prove to be financially adequate for his purposes."

"How would you feel about that?"

"I think I might like it. It's very quiet, and we

need new blood. Children would be nice." She made a point of not meeting Christa's eyes. "In lieu of that, paying guests might be acceptable and much more profitable."

Whom did they think they were fooling, Christa wondered. It was obvious that Edythe, too, had a pretty good idea of what was going on between her house guest and her nephew. She heard again that faint note of loneliness in Edythe's words that she'd picked up once or twice before. There was the same vulnerability in Edythe that she'd felt in Karl and it was just as well disguised. She admitted to herself that she was drawn to this controlled, capable woman. In fact, she wanted very much to know how Edythe felt about the things that were tearing this family apart—things that would have an immeasurable effect on Christa's future. Edythe probably considered her an outsider, but after this morning's conversation, maybe not to the extent that Christa had first thought. It might be a breach of protocol, but she went ahead anyway. "Will you be upset if Karl retains control of the winery?"

To Edythe's credit she didn't pretend not to understand. "That's a difficult question to answer. No matter how things end up, some part of me will wish they had gone the other way. Stephan told me he'd spoken with you, and I wasn't pleased. Much of what he said would have been better left unsaid. I also know you've formed an opinion of my son that's not flattering. You must realize that Stephan has had to accept a sad inheritance, and while I don't like what it's done to him, still, I can understand how he feels."

Christa started to speak but the older woman continued. "His father left him enough to live on if he is careful, but Stephan has never learned how to economize. In that respect I've failed. My brother, Karl's father, did not deserve to inherit the business—I should have received it. I had the business mind and the interest, but I was a woman and it was out of the question. Now my son is being passed over. That hurts me a second time. On the other hand, Karl is a better wine master than Stephan will ever be. I am not so blind that I can't see that. And Karl has a love of this place that surpasses even my own sometimes. It almost borders on an obsession, so I can't begrudge him his success. I wouldn't like to see the place under the control of Marcel Chenard, though that would ease things considerably for Stephan."

Christa absorbed all this slowly, and suddenly recalled something. "Stephan says it was you who saved the business when Karl's father made his mistakes."

"Yes," she said simply. "I told you, I have an excellent head for business. It's one of my few talents, I'm afraid."

"I think generosity is another," Christa interjected. "You did so much for the winery, and then to save it you turned it all over to Karl."

"That was not generosity, Fräulein Monroe. I didn't have a choice. I suppose that . . . ."

Christa reached across the table and laid her hand on Edythe's. "My name is Christa," she said.

Edythe smiled and sighed. "I'll try, but informality comes hard. I suppose, Christa," she began again, "that you find all this rather strange."

"I do," Christa admitted.

"Life in another culture takes a great deal of getting used to. I am not all that unhappy here. The castle is large and of historic interest. I take a great deal of pleasure in seeing that it's run well. And now, with all this additional work at the winery, the cooperative and our first steps into advertising, I imagine there will be something for me to do that will be more to my liking. I have to say that the thought of being involved once more is very exciting." Just then, the girl from the kitchen came in and said softly, "Frau Schröder, Herr Faulk is here to see you."

Edythe thanked her and then turned to Christa. "I've liked talking to you very much. It's been a long time since there's been another woman here whose company I've enjoyed. There have been many," she confided, "whose company I have actively avoided." Christa laughed. Edythe held her eyes for a beat more, then smiled again. "Have a nice day. I'll see you again at dinner."

THE DOOR TO THE OFFICES was open, and inside, Karl sat behind an ornate mahogany desk. His white shirt was open at the collar, a dark blue tie hanging loosely around his neck. The room was done in the colors that Christa had seen repeated throughout the castle—muted reds and blues and solemn golds. Karl was engrossed in something, but when he looked up, the smile that illuminated his face nearly dispelled her fears that she might be disturbing him. Christa felt her own pleasure at seeing him suffuse her body. It was always such a relief when she could read again in his eyes what he felt for her. *Love is such an insecure place to stand*, she thought. *It's like having your feet firmly planted on the San Andreas fault.*

Karl leaned back in his chair. "Good morning! Come in and close the door."

"Orders, orders," she grumbled, but did as he asked. Karl stood up and leaned across the desk as she bent forward to kiss him. He tried to turn the greeting into something more substantial, but the desk was too much of an impediment.

"Come around here," he invited.

"No, thanks," she said. "If I come around there, then you'll want me to sit on your lap, then you'll want to kiss me, then you'll want to do all sorts of other things and I just don't have the time right now."

"You tease," he said, and started to come around the desk after her. She backed up and opened the door, almost running into Wilhelm Tietjen.

"Am I disturbing something?" he asked quietly.

"Not at all," Karl said, sinking back down in his chair. "Miss Monroe just stopped by to say good-morning."

"Actually, I had something more than that in mind."

Karl raised his eyebrows and looked at her with an expression of such exaggerated interest that she had to laugh. If Wilhelm noticed anything, he was polite enough to keep his thoughts to himself.

"I thought I'd spend some time touring," she said, controlling a giggle. "Edythe says there are some ruins in Trier that wouldn't be too hard for me to find."

"The Porta Nigra," Wilhelm said. "You should see it if you can."

"Would you like the car?" Karl asked, reaching into his pocket to hand her his key ring. On a tattered map dug out of one of the desk drawers, he traced the route she should follow.

"That looks pretty straightforward," she said. Thanking him, she left the office, throwing him a silent kiss when she got out of Wilhelm's line of sight.

The car crept through the center of Einzell, vying with pedestrians and bicycles for every inch of roadway. There was a tractor ahead of her, leaving late for the fields, and dragging the smell of earth and fertilizer in its wake. Like the houses behind the castle, the stores of the Auguststrasse came right to the road's edge. Driving as slowly as she was, Christa was able to window-shop. Two or three times there were things she would have liked to look at more closely, but there was no place to park. Shopping in Einzell could only be done on foot or by bike. The windows of apartments above the stores were thrown wide open. Christa was sure the occupants could carry on conversations with their neighbors across the street without even raising their voices. It was probably their substitute for television, she thought. But when she looked up, she was disappointed to see that several roofs sported telltale aerials. "No place is untouched by progress," she muttered to herself.

The village ended abruptly and the road made a sharp turn down to the river, then straightened out to follow its bank. When the road branched, Christa followed the fork that took her up into the hills. Within a few miles the vineyards were replaced by rolling farmlands laid out in uniform squares. A sign indicated an access way to the autobahn, and in moments she was on the superhighway, as sterile and unappealing as superhighways anyplace in the world.

She followed the signs to Trier and drove down the main street of a small city. Suddenly, without warning, the buildings on the right ended and were replaced by lawns and bright flowers and a massive black structure that made her catch her breath. It was the Porta Nigra, the Black Gate. She watched it recede through the rearview mirror and then searched for a parking space.

The ruin was four stories tall at its highest point and towered one hundred feet above the ground. At one time it must have been part of the wall that surrounded the city. All that remained now was a pair of immense arches side by side, flanked by solid walls of stone stretching like wings to the right and left. One arch was for entering, one for exiting. The Romans knew about traffic control even then, Christa mused. Above the remains of the walls and gates, two additional stories rose, consisting of a series of smaller, window-sized arches and columns. The stone had a rosy cast, overlaid by a black patina that had taken two thousand years to accumulate.

Christa approached the ruin head-on, walking along the path that led from the road. A sense of wonder slowed her steps so that just before she entered it she stopped. Hesitantly, she touched the stones, warm from the sun, and saw how intricately they fitted together. She tried to accept how long ago the gate had been built, how long ago these stones had been laid in place. Raised to protect a Roman city, it was also a thing of massive beauty, graced by columns, raised stone, and vertical and horizontal decorative lines. It exuded power and authority.

She almost had to push herself to start through it. The narrow passageways were like short tunnels and it was cool and dark inside them. Thirty feet above her the ceilings of the arches soared, the stones chiseled to curve in perfect symmetry. Historical ruins were nothing new to Christa. She'd visited the Old North Church, Bunker Hill, Betsy Ross's house, those landmarks of America; but this was more than that. This was a legacy left to mark the advancing of the human race. No wonder it was called Imperial Rome, she thought, if Romans were erecting things like this while the rest of the world lived in huts. Christa closed her eyes and could almost feel the chariots pass, wishing she had waited for Karl, needing someone to share this with.

She was tempted to go back to the castle immediately so that she could tell Karl what she'd ex-

perienced, then laughed at herself. He would hardly
appreciate having his meetings interrupted by the
earth-shattering news that the Romans had built one
hell of a gate in Trier. As a matter of fact, there
wasn't anything she could think of that Karl would
be interested in hearing right now. All his energies
and thoughts were centered on the winery, and even
their banter this morning hadn't hidden that. She
was pricked by a sharp awareness of how left out
Edythe had felt.

Continuing through the passageway, she emerged
into a sun-filled, paved courtyard filled with tables
protected by red-and-white-striped umbrellas. People sat there drinking coffee and reading news-
papers, oblivious of the marvel just a few yards
away. Christa sat at one of the tables herself, but her
attention was still on the ruin. It was older than the
castle. When Conrad Lothair had been supervising
the laying of the first tier of stone, this gate had already been standing a thousand years. The thought
was unexpectedly depressing. The stark Roman ruin
had touched something deep inside Christa. It was
more than a world removed from Boston, and suddenly she had a deep longing for the noises and
smells of home, the well-known and understood
clamor of Commonwealth Avenue. What was she
doing here in a place whose rules and regulations
weren't part of her? She looked around helplessly,
but nowhere could she find a sense of belonging.
There were no well-loved, friendly objects nearby.
All she had here was Karl, and an icy fear crept
through her. For the first time she allowed herself to

really consider what it would be like if she stayed. Nothing means more to him than that winery, Stephan had told her. Edythe had said that his love for the place bordered on an obsession. Suppose Christa and Karl got married and she found this to be true?

Stop it, she told herself. *You've just been alone too long.* Two days with nothing to do and she was falling apart. What if she married Karl and had *years* of nothing to do? How many people would be willing to hire a consultant who had trouble with the language and no feeling at all for the customs? She stared at the gate again. There were other Roman relics in Trier, but she'd lost any desire to see them, nor had she any desire to go back to the castle where Karl would be involved and Edythe would be busy and Stephan would probably be the only one available to talk to. Her thoughts brought her such a heavy feeling of depression, it was as if someone had draped her in mourning. *Stop it*, she told herself again. She was just having a long-overdue and rather severe attack of homesickness. She forced herself to get up and get on with her day, and spent the afternoon in Trier. There was a lot to see, some of it very beautiful, but she could summon little enthusiasm. Finally, late in the afternoon, she headed back to the castle.

11

CHRISTA'S MOOD LASTED all through dinner, and Karl did nothing to dispel it. He and Wilhelm talked animatedly about the winery; no amount of effort on anyone's part could change the subject. Halfway into the meal Stephan excused himself, saying he'd had all the talk he could take, and a moment later they heard his Mercedes speed down the drive. Christa saw the look of unhappiness on Edythe's face and tried to catch her eye to tell her she understood, but Edythe controlled her feelings and joined the conversation between Karl and Wilhelm. Under the table Karl's hand rested on Christa's knee. He smiled at her often and asked her opinion on marketing approaches. She came up with some ideas but found it difficult, as her mind was on other things. Karl didn't seem to mind her distraction. Up until now, he told her, she had always had something very definite to say. Never mind, he soothed, there would be time soon enough for her to do some serious thinking.

When they had finished the dessert of fruit and *crème fraîche*, Karl excused himself and closeted Wilhelm and himself again in his office. Again, Christa and Edythe were left sitting at the table.

"You look tired," Edythe said. "Sight-seeing can do that to you."

"How long do you think they'll be?"

"Quite a while, I'm afraid. This is a busy time. Would you like to take a walk? I was thinking of going down to the river for a breath of fresh air before it gets dark."

Christa sighed. "Thank you, but I am tired, and I wouldn't be very good company. I think I'll just go upstairs." She folded her napkin and started across the room, her heels making a hollow sound on the worn Oriental rug. "If you see Karl, would you tell him I've gone to bed, Frau Schröder?"

"Please don't look so sad, my dear, Karl would be with you if he could. And Christa, you may call me Edythe."

"I know he would. It's just that he's all I've got here—I suddenly realized that today. I'll feel better in the morning. Good night, Edythe," she said smiling softly, testing the name.

MORNING, HOWEVER, brought no improvement. "Why didn't you come to me last night?" Christa asked Karl as they lingered alone in the dining room.

"It was so late, *Liebchen*, I didn't want to disturb you. Are you getting bored? Would you like me to have one of the men drive you in to . . . ."

"No," she snapped, cutting him off. "I take it that means you're going to be busy all day again. I'm not complaining, Karl," she added. "I know you have work to do. I just wish I had some. Do you think I could help Edythe with anything?"

"Why don't you ask her?" He leaned over to kiss Christa lightly on the cheek. Then, changing his mind, he touched his lips to hers in a kiss that, had she allowed it, could have developed into something more. "I will see you tonight," he promised, his eyes searching her face before he kissed her again, "and now I'd better leave while I still have some willpower left."

What, she wondered, did Edythe do all day? What did it take to run the castle? She would not even know where to start looking for her. Christa filled her coffee cup for the third time and carried it out to the terrace. From the far side of the hedges she could hear Edythe and Stephan talking. Stephan's words were clipped and angry, Edythe's soft and conciliatory.

"I have no desire to compromise." Stephan's voice suddenly sounded very clearly, then dropped again. A moment later his car started up and left the grounds. Christa heard Edythe in the dining room, and turned to stand in the doorway.

"Was that Stephan's car I just heard leaving?"

"Yes, he asked me to give you his apology. He left rather suddenly and had no time to say goodbye." *A white lie*, Christa thought, *the kind we all indulge in to keep the surface of our lives a little smoother.* If this had been Boston, if Edythe had been an American, Christa would have given her a hug, would have found some way to touch her to let her know she understood the other woman's pain. But this was Einzell, and Christa stayed where she was.

She watched as Edythe went through one of the

drawers in a large buffet. She removed a tablecloth and napkins, laid them on top of the piece and turned to leave.

"Is there anything I can do for you, Edythe?" Christa asked, hesitating a little over the name, still conscious of all that was involved in her right to use it. "I seem to be at loose ends again."

"Oh, my dear, I am sorry. I won't be at the castle for most of the day and there really isn't anything you could do without me. Perhaps one of the men might be able to drive you...."

"I've been through that already with Karl," Christa returned sharply, then softened her tone. None of this was Edythe's fault. "I'd just as soon stay around here in case Karl has some free time. Maybe I'll walk to the Auguststrasse and do some shopping. Is there anything I can pick up for you?"

"Shampoo," Edythe said. "I realized this morning that I need some. It will save my making an extra stop. Thank you. I'll see you at dinner then?"

CHRISTA HAD TOYED WITH THE IDEA of calling Elena, but that would have indicated an intention of pursuing a friendship, and she wasn't able to promise that. She wasn't sure of her intentions at all.... Instead, she walked desultorily through the shops. She tried on a short jacket in a bright cornflower blue and on impulse bought it for her mother. Her mood brightened a little as she thought how her mother would enjoy wearing it. She hadn't bought any presents for anyone back home, hadn't even thought of it. She wondered if it was an omen that the subject was on her mind now. Was she finally beginning to realize that she would, after all, be going home? She forced herself to find something for her father and settled on a hand-carved pipe. She bought her grandmother a cuckoo clock, knowing she would love the silliness of it, and for Elizabeth a delicate set of Bavarian-made demitasses for a wedding gift.

Then Christa brought her purchases back to the castle and ate a lonely lunch in the dining room.

Had she really ever thought she would fit in here? How could Karl not have realized how out of place she would end up being? He couldn't possibly have assumed she would be happy shopping and reading her days away, could he? Didn't he know her at all?

Sitting next to Karl at dinner that evening was agony. He persisted in acting as if nothing were wrong, as if nothing had changed, and she was gracious enough to understand that he was not aware it had. Pleading a headache, she escaped to her room where she did in fact take two aspirin and lie down. Her mind blessedly blocked the fact that somehow during this long, empty day, a decision had been made. There was no sound from inside the castle, so her ears followed the town's preparation for night. The last of the tractors chugged in from the fields and passed under her window. She heard the high chatter of children, and the concerned voices of mothers collecting them for the evening. The children all seemed so happy here, the women so relaxed. It would have been a lovely place to raise a family had things been different. She had dreamed of taking their children down to the river to feed the swans and watch the boats as Karl had done with his father, but this time the memories they made would be happy ones. Now there would be no memories at all, at least none that she would care to hold on to.

The muffled knock on her small balcony door finally came. She had been expecting it. She lifted her unwilling body from the bed and jacked the door up so that it could be opened. They had been kidding themselves, those castle builders, if they thought a door and step could protect their women. A simple knock from the right hand was all it took to shatter their defenses.

"Are you better?" Karl asked her softly, brushing past and putting something down on the table before clicking on her lamp. He turned to see her drawn face in the light. "*Liebchen*, you really are sick."

She ran her hand through her hair and attempted a smile. "I'm okay, just a little weary."

"Too weary for me to stay?"

"No, I want you to stay. We need to talk."

"I wanted tonight to be a celebration," he said, and she saw that what he had placed on the table was a bottle of wine and two glasses. "I have a lot to tell you."

He needed someone to share his victory, and she couldn't deny him that. "And I want to hear it." She sat cross-legged on the bed and forced some brightness into her smile. "Shoot," she said.

He looked at her quizzically, then laughed.

"Right, I'm shooting. I was very good. I had that meeting in the palm of my hand."

"I expected nothing less."

"I gave them all the facts and figures, and I had an answer for every question." He walked around the room as he talked. "Why am I still so keyed up? It must be a reaction. I knew after Fabiani said he was with us that it would work out, but I guess I was afraid to believe. Then today Paul was at the meeting. He's changed his mind—he's with us, too. I spent a lot of time talking to him over the past two days, and it's paid off." Karl sat down next to Christa on the bed and kissed her happily. "This is the first time, the very first time that I actually feel that I'm in control. _I'm_ setting the course the winery will take. It's a good feeling."

He kissed her again. If he noticed any problem with her response, he didn't mention it. His eyes were the blazing blue of a summer sky. _Do you know how many people have that combination? How many people really mean it when they say they want to win?_ Vera Eason's voice was soft in her memory. _Not many_, Christa had said. But Karl was one of them.

He was up and walking again. "We have to seriously consider the future."

"I have been," she said. "I've spent the past two days thinking about it."

Something about her voice warned him. "And?"

"I've come to the conclusion that it won't work."

He stood perfectly still. "What are you saying?"

"I'm saying that I can't give up my country, my

job, my family, everything, to live here with you."
She'd no sooner begun than her words caught on a
sob. Karl stared at her disbelievingly and she
looked away. "I think I knew it from the beginning."

"Wait a minute." There was an angry flush on his
cheeks. "When did all this happen? I had the impression that you understood what I was trying to
do, that you wanted me to succeed."

"I did, I do."

"But you don't want to be part of it?"

She swallowed hard, and took a deep breath. She
could try to explain to him how she felt, but she
knew she'd never get through it all without breaking down, so she simply said, "No, I don't."

"Then what the hell's been going on here for the
past couple of weeks?"

"Please, don't."

"What's been going on between us? A little diver-
sion so you could spend your vacation in a castle?"

"Stop it!"

"For someone who doesn't want to be part of my
life you certainly threw yourself into our encounters." His voice was cold.

She put her hands over her ears to block out the
sound of it. "This has nothing to do with what went
on between us." Her voice was unnaturally high.
She had not planned what she would say to him,
nor had she planned to sob her way through. She
was upset at her loss of control. Karl pulled her
from the bed and held her tightly.

"Sweetheart, don't cry," he begged, kissing her

face, her eyes, her mouth. "I don't know what this is all about but we can handle it. *Liebchen, Liebchen....*" His hands on her back pressed her close to him while he rocked her gently back and forth.

She pushed away, wiped her eyes ineffectively with the back of her hand and drew a shuddering breath. She was handling this all wrong. She would never be able to explain it to him now. Steeling herself against the look of hurt in his eyes, she started again.

"Karl," she began slowly, "listen to me. When you first suggested I come here, you said it was because you wanted me to see for myself what you were fighting to hold on to. You wanted me to understand. I do. I really do. I see that you have no choice. You have to try to hold it all together for as long as you can. Sometimes inanimate things have a life of their own, and certain people must keep them going. I think that's what's happened to you."

"That's part of it," he said. "But there's more. For years I've listened to people talk about my parents. Stephan has always been willing to tell me what a bitch my mother was, how weak my father was. I swore to my father on his deathbed that I would put the winery back under von Klee control. I swore that I would not lose it to the French a second time. I told him I would save his honor. And I've done that." His voice was fierce.

"I understand, and I'm happy for you. But that's your triumph, not mine. Mine would have been convincing you to come back to Boston with me. I can't live here. I've tried not to face that, but now I have to. It was wonderful being here with you, but I can't ignore the facts any longer. What we've had is not what we'll have if I marry you. These past few days have shown me that. After you give most of your time to the winery, how much will be left for me?"

"I don't know," he said honestly. "All the rest, however much that is."

"Suppose it isn't enough? Suppose I end up like your mother, doing all sorts of cruel things because I didn't get what I had hoped, because there's really no place for me here."

"But there is a place for you. With four more vineyards to process, I'm going to be spending most of my time in the sheds. I'll need someone in the office, someone to handle the advertising and the relationship between us and New York, and all the other places that will be clamoring for our wine."

"That person should be Edythe."

"Edythe?" His face was blank. "She wouldn't be interested in working with me."

"Oh, Karl, for heaven's sake, of course she would," Christa exclaimed. "Talk to her. She loves this place as much as you do, and she's a big enough person to bury the past. Stephan is her son but she knows you're the better wine master. She deserves to be included. Why, if it hadn't been for her, the winery wouldn't be here at all."

"You're wrong," argued Karl. "There are too many bitter memories of the winery for Edythe to want to be part of it again."

"Oh, Karl, please, think about it," Christa urged.

"Perhaps. But right now, I'm interested in us. We're discussing our lives, not hers." Karl reached for her, his fingers biting into the soft flesh below her shoulders.

"Do you love me?" he asked, intent on her face.

She closed her eyes and refused to answer. He shook her sharply and she looked up to see the fear and anger in his eyes.

"Answer me," he demanded.

"I love you, of course," she admitted. "But it doesn't change anything. You have your work, your life, your friends. I'd have nothing."

"You'd have my love," he pointed out quietly.

"Is that enough? And for how long? Can you guarantee that I'll have it for the rest of my life? I'm sorry, but this is all too nebulous."

"I'll tell you this one more time," he said, his eyes glittering like broken glass. "What I feel for you is real. I had hoped that when you saw the winery and realized what I was trying to do, you would want to help me. However, whether you want to help me or not, I can't give up doing what I must. But the winery is only one part of my life. You are the other, and no matter what my involvement with the business is, it has no bearing on this thing that exists between us."

"This *thing*?" Christa pounced on the word as if it were her vindication. "See? You're not sure what it is either, no matter what you say." There was almost a note of triumph in her voice, as if at last she were proving herself, proving that her decision not to stay was a reasonable one.

"You're right, I'm not. How can anyone ever be sure about what exists between two people? You can only hope that what you think is there really is."

"And that's enough to build a life on?"

"It has to be," he said. "No one ever has much more."

"Yes, they do. They have their jobs and families and friends. Here I'd have only you, and the hope that you're being honest when you say you love me."

"What happened to all that righteous indignation that you used to throw at me about my not wanting to stay with you? It's different now when the sacrifices are on *your* side."

"You didn't make those sacrifices either," she shot back at him.

"I couldn't," he retorted, his voice raw with frustration. "I thought that's what this trip was about. I thought you understood that I didn't have the luxury of a choice." He sat wearily on the bed and ran his hand through his hair. "It won't always be so one-sided. In the beginning the sacrifices will be yours, but just until I get things going, just until the cooperative is secure. I had hoped that we'd be working at it together."

"It will always be one-sided." Her fear of being unable to stand firm made her voice hard. "I will always be living in your world, under your direction, meeting your goals. That's not what I had planned for my life."

The silence dragged on and on until Christa

thought she would scream. When she met Karl's eyes they were expressionless, as if a curtain had been drawn over them. He got up slowly from the bed, like an old man whose joints ached. "I misjudged you and I misconstrued our relationship," he said when he was standing. "It's not entirely your fault. I expected too much. I think you're right—people never do love enough. You'd think I'd have learned that by now. I don't know why I thought my future would be any different from my past."

It's better not to be responsible for someone else, she told him silently. *It's better to just handle your own life, and then when things go wrong you have only yourself to blame.*

"I apologize for my mistake," he said. His control was frightening in its completeness. He walked over to the table and fingered the bottle of wine he had brought in with him. Then, grasping it by the neck, he swung it viciously and sent it crashing against the wall. It smashed with an explosive sound and its contents bled down the plaster and seeped into the rug.

Christa drew a sharp breath, but Karl, without looking at her, walked out, slamming the hall door after him. When she was sure he was gone, she gave in to her anger. There was nothing fair about life. What Machiavellian casting director had handed her and Karl their parts, then sat back laughing while they struggled with their lines?

I was right, she told herself over and over again. *I would never see my parents. My children would never know their maternal grandparents. They would think other families were like this one.*

He misjudged me, he misconstrued our relationship—I'll bet! I wonder how much of his disappointment is because he loves me and how much is because I know more about advertising than he does. How much of his concern is for that damned winery? A lot, I'll bet. A whole damn lot.

It felt so good to blame him, to lay this mess at his feet. She forced herself to remember how many times he'd brought up the business about Caldwell and what she'd done there. She recalled how concerned he had been that she set up a meeting between him and Lewis and Loman.

The hell with all of them. She wanted her dirty, noisy city of Boston. She wanted her parents, open and honest as Karl's family could never be. She wanted her flighty old grandmother and her septuagenarian poker partners. And if she ever did get married, and she very much doubted she would, it would be to a nice, safe American boy, whose past didn't stretch back any farther than his birthday.

She glared at the stain on the wall. The carpet was probably ruined, and Edythe would blame her for that. Let her. Tomorrow she'd be out of here, shaking the dust of Einzell from feet that couldn't move fast enough. She marched into the bathroom and brought the wastebasket back with her, then knelt to pick up the pieces of glass. There were a lot of them—small sharp slivers, shards of a promise that had shattered before it could be kept.

The only large piece of glass was the section where the label was pasted. She picked it up carefully and turned it over to read it. The only thing she could tell clearly was that it was not a von Klee wine. That surprised her. Carrying the fragment to the table she held it under the lamp. The label was old and faded, and she rubbed the dust away gingerly. It was a Burgundy, and the date on it was the year she was born.

She lowered herself to the chair and stared at the piece of glass in her hand, and all the unpleasant words that had been spoken that evening settled down slowly to lie in messy piles on the floor. She knew what the wine had been meant to convey.

He loves me—and I love him. But it wouldn't have been enough, she told herself fiercely. *There isn't always enough. I couldn't have stayed.* Christa pleaded her case to the empty room, brushing angrily at the tears that spilled down her face. She got up and crossed quickly to the armoire, pulling her clothes from it. She had to leave now, right now, even if it meant spending the night at a hotel. When the armoire was empty she yanked out her drawers, dumping their contents haphazardly on the bed. "I am not running away," she assured herself aloud as she sorted the clothes into ragged piles. There was just no more reason to stay.

She would find Edythe and give her some excuse for leaving so precipitately. And Karl? If she saw him again, would she be able to do what she felt she must?

She pulled a sheet of notepaper from the desk drawer and wrote, "I'm sorry, my love. It would never have worked." Then, Christa wrote Karl's name on the envelope, sealed it and left it on the desk.

12

IT HAD BEEN SPRING when she left Boston, and now it was summer. Claiborne Street had settled in for a siege of hot weather. Christa had come directly from the airport to her apartment, holed up for two days and then coaxed her Datsun to make the long drive to Leicester to see her parents.

She had been away long enough that they didn't suspect she had cut the visit short. They simply thought her vacation was over.

"We should go over there, Patrick," her mother said. "Karl has invited us a dozen times."

Her father raised his eyebrows at Christa. He and she had been to Einzell and knew that the rosy picture Christa painted of life at the Castle von Klee embroidered slightly on the truth.

"I'd wait," Christa suggested. "Things are busy there right now."

"Oh, I didn't mean tomorrow," Peggy Monroe said, "I just meant someday."

"Like someday we're going to sell this house?" her husband teased her.

"Kind of like that," she agreed.

Patrick leaned back in his lawn chair and rested his feet on the low stone wall surrounding the patio.

"Look at that," he said, pointing to the riot of flowers blooming beyond the pond. "Bet you didn't see anything prettier than that in Germany."

"Germany is another world," Christa answered.

"Not really." Her father puffed on his pipe, took it out of his mouth to admire it, then continued to smoke contentedly.

"Please, dad, not one of your lectures on what a small world it really is." She was sorry after she'd said it, for her voice had a sharpness she hadn't intended.

"Well, it is," he replied, somewhat miffed. "But I won't point it out to you if you'd rather not hear it."

"Are you coming down with something?" Peggy asked Christa. "You're certainly not yourself."

Christa looked out over the pond and tried not to remember what had once happened there. "I'm still tired from the time change. It was probably a mistake to come up here so soon." But she had wanted to see them badly, wanted to reattach her ties, to settle in and belong again. The two days she had spent in her apartment had convinced her that she needed more than just being in Boston to bring things back to the way they had been.

"Don't be silly," her father chided, "it's about time you came. We haven't seen you in a couple of months, and we'd rather have you crabby than not at all."

"Thanks," she said dryly. "A lot of my time before the trip was spent entertaining Karl." She congratulated herself on how easily she could say his name.

"I always thought there might have been something between you two." Her mother glanced at her.

"You always think there's something between me and somebody," Christa chided gently.

"I guess I do," her mother admitted.

"That would have been a nice way to round things out," her father offered. "You and Karl."

"You just finished complaining that you never see me. How would you like it if I lived in Germany?"

"Karl gets to the States pretty often, and it would give us a reason to travel. Right, Peg?"

"Actually, it might be very nice," his wife agreed. "We could have our own suite at the castle and visit whenever we liked. Can't you imagine Dean Welton's face if we told him we were spending Christmas with our daughter at her castle?" Peggy laughed at the idea.

"Could we please get off this subject? The castle comes equipped with Karl and his family and they're not all that wonderful. They have some rather serious faults, not the least of which is an alarming amount of egotism."

"You could have misread them," Patrick ventured. "I've known—"

"What's new with Grandma?" Christa interrupted, ignoring the look that flashed between her parents. *What's the matter with her*, they seemed to be asking each other. *People who come back from vacations are supposed to be happy and relaxed, and Christa is anything but that.*

"Nothing much," her mother said, going along

with the change of subject. "She's still seeing Mr. Phillips."

"The one with the whopping social security check?"

"I think this may be serious. She's kind of lonely, though she'd never admit it. I'd like to see her married again, wouldn't you, Patrick?"

"At her age I don't think it matters too much."

"Of course it does," her mother insisted. "You get awfully selfish with only yourself to think about."

"Was that a dig at me?" Christa asked defensively.

"Christa, you must have lost a layer of skin in Germany. I've never known you to be so sensitive. It wasn't a dig at anyone, it was a simple statement of fact. People who live alone tend to get selfish."

"I can't imagine what it must be like to live with someone day in and day out." She said the words softly, expecting her mother to answer, in her usual breezy way, that there was nothing to it. Hadn't they been doing it for almost thirty-five years? Instead, Peggy let a little silence grow.

"It isn't the easiest thing in the world," she replied, her voice serious. "Sometimes it's downright difficult, but never impossible." She leaned over to lay an affectionate hand on her husband's knee.

"How did you and dad know that you wanted to spend the rest of your life together?"

"Oh, Lord, when you put it like that it sounds so ponderous. It was just nicer to be together than it was to be separated."

"Weren't you scared?"

"Petrified," Patrick said.

"Then why did you do it?"

"Like your mother said, it was better to be scared together than scared apart."

"But people change," Christa said.

"That's true. I'm certainly not the man I used to be." He waited for someone to refute the statement.

"You're better," Peggy consoled him.

"Took you long enough to say it," he grumbled.

"You are better," she said. "You're kinder, more patient, less demanding, and if I hadn't married you then, I'd marry you now."

A breeze rippled the surface of the pond and clouds piled up in the west, promising a storm.

"It's funny, isn't it, when you stop to think about it." Patrick's voice was distracted. "Why *do* people get married? I've considered the problem on and off for years. The closest I can come to explaining it is that somehow, with some people, you add up to more, you're better than the sum of your individual parts. When you meet someone who makes you realize that, you grab her—" he reached over to take his wife's hand "—and you hang on for dear life."

"A mizpah coin," Christa said softly, and her father chuckled at the simile.

Her mother examined her closely, probing for some explanation of her daughter's strange behavior and the rather odd discussion she had precipitated. Knowing what a romantic her mother was, Christa knew what conclusion she would come to. This time she would inadvertently hit on the truth. Christa also knew that for now, at least, seeing how testy her daughter was behaving, Peggy would keep her conclusions to herself.

THEY WERE GLAD TO SEE HER at Caldwell, and Christa prepared to take up where she had left off—only none of it seemed important anymore. She tried, she really did, but the frenzy that gripped the staff as to the relative merits of one plaid over another failed to reach her.

Even lunch with Bob Fairfax did nothing to start her creative juices flowing. After trying unsuccessfully to engage her interest in some ads he was preparing for a Christmas spread, he stopped talking and watched her pick at her food. In an offhand way he asked what her impression had been of the von Klee winery. He'd had a letter from Karl saying they were going to go ahead with the campaign.

Attentive for the first time since they sat down, Christa asked who his contact would be.

"Von Klee himself, I guess. I just assumed it would be him. He didn't offer any other name."

"I suppose this sort of thing can be handled by mail," she commented, holding her breath a little.

"Most of it, but he did say he would fly in for the final consultations whenever we're ready."

She didn't want to know that. She didn't want to think about Karl being in Boston, ever. "Why are you telling me all this stuff about Karl? He's not my concern. All I did was introduce you to the man."

"Sorry," Bob said, surprised.

"My concern is Caldwell, Limited," she further emphasized, and having said that, went back to picking at her food. Finally she pleaded a headache and excused herself.

ELIZABETH WAS THE HARDEST of all for Christa to deal with, because she alone knew what the situation had been with Karl. At first Elizabeth greeted her with eyes bright with excitement. "How was it? Did you have a good time? Do you realize you didn't even send me one postcard?"

"I didn't send anybody one." In the beginning she had been too happy to think about postcards and at the end she had been too sad.

"Start at the beginning." Elizabeth settled herself in Christa's velvet wing chair. "From the moment you got off the plane."

"Well, the country's very beautiful," Christa began.

"Forget that. I'll concede that Germany is a picture, I want to know about you and Karl."

Christa ran her hand through her hair and rubbed the back of her neck.

"Why do I have this awful sensation in the pit of my stomach?" Elizabeth asked.

"I have no idea." Christa got up quickly and walked to the windows. "Maybe you get too involved in other people's lives. It's not a good habit to get into. Obviously it gives you indigestion."

"Here we go again." Elizabeth sighed. "I'm going to make a stab in the dark. Things did not go well for you and Karl."

Christa pulled up the corners of her mouth in a parody of a smile and shook her head.

"He wasn't very nice to you."

"He was very attentive."

"You didn't like the castle."

"The castle was beautiful." Even now, damn it, she had to watch that her voice didn't betray her.

"Karl didn't want you to stay?"

"*I* didn't want to stay. And before you start coming down hard, let me tell you something. You have absolutely no idea what is involved in loving someone who lives in another country, another culture."

"That's garbage, Christa, and you know it."

"I do *not* know it." Christa's voice was steel.

"Listen, Christa, if I had to name one person who would not be frightened by the idea of making a drastic change in her living conditions it would be you. You're very self-contained, you take all of you wherever you go. Now, I could see myself having a problem. I'm so diffuse I'd have to take half my world with me if I moved. But not you. Why don't you tell me what really happened?"

"Why don't you mind your own business?" Christa threw the words at her, regretting them immediately.

"Tell you what, why don't we just forget it?" Elizabeth said stiffly, getting up and starting for the door. "If you ever feel like talking, give me a call."

"Wait, Elizabeth, please. I didn't mean it. I'm so sorry. I'm snapping at everyone. If I tell you what happened, will you promise not to lecture me? I'm really not in the market for advice."

"Okay, Christa, no lectures, no advice."

So Christa told her about Germany, about the

vineyards and the castle, about Karl's family and about Karl. "He says he loves me, and he thinks he's telling the truth, but it's the vineyards he *really* cares about. If he had to make a choice, he'd choose them. I'd always be on the outside looking in."

"That's too bad," Elizabeth said finally. "I'm really sorry to hear it." She brushed some nonexistent lint from her lap, started to say something and changed her mind. Instead, she stood up. "Well, I guess that's that and I'd better get going. I have some things to do before I get ready for bed." She walked to the door. "I'm glad you're back. I've missed you."

Christa watched her in amazement. "Is that all you're going to say?"

"You told me not to lecture you, to keep my opinions to myself, and I can't commiserate with you because I think you're dead wrong. So I'm leaving, because if I stayed the pressure of keeping my mouth shut would blow the top of my head off." Her voice had risen several decibels. "You are the biggest fool I have ever met, Christa Monroe!" The apartment door slammed after her.

CHRISTA DISCOVERED a fascinating thing about life— it went on, regardless of whether people cared or not. Each morning her alarm sounded and she went through the motions of existence: she ate, met Elizabeth, went to work and came home again.

She sat at her desk for eight hours a day, took care of whatever came before her and took care of it well. She made decisions, implemented changes, did some research on a possible new client and felt totally unfulfilled. That had never happened to her before. She had always been able to summon up some feeling of self-worth after a good day's work—but not anymore.

Time was not a static dimension. Some days went by shrouded in a fog, and she had no recollection of them at all. Other days passed so painfully slowly that she was aware of each minute. She was sure the hours multiplied themselves geometrically and she checked the mirror frequently for signs of aging and any similarity to Vera Eason's eyes.

"You don't look well," Elizabeth grumbled at her, resolutely keeping her thoughts on the reason to herself.

A recurring dream began to haunt Christa. In it, she was perched precariously in a high place. She knew, in her dream consciousness, that she couldn't stay there but there was no way down that she could see.

Someone was standing far below, and though she could hardly make him out she knew it was Karl. "Jump," he told her. "The air currents will keep you afloat."

She knew he was wrong. She knew that air currents, like love, could not always be depended on. But Karl kept insisting. Finally she jumped. Initially the updraft caught her, blowing her dress tight against her legs, and she experienced weightless freedom for the first time.

Then things changed. She could feel the air support lessen, and she began to fall, plummeting helplessly toward the ground. She woke just before she hit, drenched in sweat, clutching the sheets.

Then one day Christa was walking along Commonwealth Avenue to an appointment with Vera Eason. Ahead of her in the crowd she saw a tall slender man striding along the pavement as if he owned it and everything on it. His hair was blond and slightly longer than it should have been. His neck was slender, but the shoulders beneath his short-sleeved white shirt were well-muscled and substantial. Her heart stopped for two full beats. She picked up the pace of her steps, not so much to catch up with him as just to keep him in sight.

She dodged between people and ran across streets when the light was against her, moving almost without volition. Her hands tingled at the thought that she could reach out and touch him if she wanted to. There was a feeling inside her of an engine laboriously coming to life, like her Datsun on a cold December morning. Gears began to mesh, nerve endings reattached themselves. Her heart was beating so hard she could hear it; her breathing was rapid. Her entire body seemed to have come alive with a jolt.

"Karl." She said his name out loud, but softly. She was finally within ten feet of him. But now she could see that the hair wasn't the right shade of blond, that the neck was a little too slender and the walk, the set of the shoulders, not right. When he turned to enter a building she realized she'd never seen the man before. It was the same thing she used to do at eighteen; she hadn't progressed at all. She entered the building after him and leaned against a wall, feeling whatever resources she had just summoned drain out of her. She pulled herself together and made it to the restaurant. For the first time in their association, Vera was there first. They went through the ritual of ordering drinks and then Vera got down to business. Christa kept dragging her mind back to the problems at hand, but each time Vera paused, waiting for a comment, Christa seemed to be a million miles away.

"I don't have time for this, sweetie," Vera said. "Do you want to call me when you're back in touch?"

"I'm sorry, Vera." Christa flushed. "I know this is unforgivable. Would you mind going over things one more time and I swear I'll pay attention."

Instead Vera sat back in her chair and looked at Christa. "You might pay attention, but your heart won't be in it. You can't generate much creativity under those conditions. Are you ill?"

"Not physically. I've had to make a difficult decision and I'm still learning to live with it."

"Maybe if it's that hard to live with, it's the wrong decision."

"No, it was right."

"I'm glad to hear you say that, because we're talking about the German wine grower, aren't we? It wasn't so hard to figure out. You went to Germany on top of the world and came back looking like you'd fallen off. I warned you that friends, the male ones, can wreak havoc with your goals. You don't need him, Christa. You've got a fine future ahead of you if you're careful. I told you once before you can't afford too many mistakes, and letting your personal life intrude on your business life is a big one. Now go home—you look awful. Call me when you've put this thing to rest; I have a few more names to pass on to you."

CHRISTA'S BEDROOM WAS QUIET, but the light was wrong. It was two o'clock Tuesday afternoon light, and she shouldn't have been there to see it. She took off her dress and shoes and left them where they fell, stretching herself out stiffly on the bed. Whom was she kidding? Whom was she trying to fool? For three weeks she had been telling herself things were getting back to normal—all she had to do was hang in there. Did she consider that lunch with Vera normal? Was it normal to follow a man blocks out of her way and then fall apart when it turned out he was a stranger? The past weeks had been awful, and the months that stretched ahead showed every indication of being the same. This was nothing like the first time. Bad as that had been, this was worse. This time she could take no comfort in hating Karl. She pulled on a light shift and padded barefoot into the hall, descended one flight and sat on the bottom step. It would be hours before Elizabeth came home.

"LOCKED OUT?" Elizabeth asked when she saw her.

Christa shook her head. "I need to talk," she said.

Elizabeth silently unlocked her door and stood back while Christa went in. Elizabeth kicked off her shoes, peeled off her stockings, turned the air conditioner up two notches and sat down across from Christa.

"I don't know where to start," Christa said.

"Well, let's go back to 'the country was really beautiful' and go on from there."

"Elizabeth, I'm miserable. Everything seemed so clear in Einzell. I'd be better off without him. I'd have my own life, my own work. In Boston I may not be much, but I am somebody. In Einzell I'd be nobody, living within the borders Karl set."

"Would they be such awful borders? From what you've said, there'd be more than enough for you to do. It's not so bad to belong, to fit yourself into someone else's life. It's a two-way street. You give, but you also get. What's so wonderful about being alone?"

Christa tried to conjure up herself as another Vera Eason. "At least you're always sure."

"Sure of what?"

"I don't know." The picture of herself strong and alone crumbled. "Something."

"I can't help you, Christa. You're on your own with this one. You were right when you told me I didn't know what I was talking about. I have no idea what it means to give up everything and move to another country."

"Would you do it for Mark?"

"He wouldn't ask me. He's even less daring than I am. I guess that's why we love each other."

"Why couldn't I have fallen in love with someone who'd be satisfied with a nine-to-five job and a house in Brookline?"

"You had opportunities and you weren't interested. You need bigger challenges than that. But this one's awfully big. You're the only one who can decide if it's too big."

"You think the problem is me, not Karl."

"Oh, Christa, how could I know that? But I can tell you that, given a choice, I'd choose love every time, over everything else."

SHE MADE IT as far as the top step of her landing and then sat down again. Elizabeth would choose love, Vera would choose independence. She was neither Elizabeth nor Vera. She wanted more than either one of them. She wanted it all, and no one ever really got that. Karl had said that not everything was black and white. Choices were like that. Sometimes you had to move into a gray area, mixing what you could and couldn't have. She had been afraid to love him, and she had been right to be afraid—part of her had always known what the cost of love could be. Now she was being asked to pay the price. It was almost midnight when she finally left the stairs and went to bed. She slept soundly, dreamlessly, for the first time in days.

When dawn turned her windows milky Christa woke, fished her small suitcase out from under the bed and packed. She wouldn't need much; even if her trip was successful she wouldn't be there long. Her hands were unsteady as she pressed the clothing into place. She took a shower, then sat staring at the telephone until the clock in her living room struck nine. She called a travel agency, reserved a seat on the six o'clock flight to Frankfurt, and offered up a small prayer that Karl still wanted her.

Christa carried her suitcase to work and, without explaining where she was going, told Katie she had been called away on a family emergency. Katie was too sensitive to question her further. The day plodded on. At four o'clock Christa left the office and rode to the airport, refusing to allow herself to think about what she was doing.

The flight was uneventful, and she landed in Frankfurt at nine in the morning under cloudy skies. She hired a car, threw her suitcase in the back seat and headed for Einzell. It wasn't until she reached the river and turned along its bank that the enormity of what she was doing hit her. Her throat turned dry, her hands clammy.

The vineyards had changed in the brief time she had been gone. They'd leafed out and lost that bristling, threatening look. She could see small clusters of grapes hanging close to the vines. Entering the village, she was lost in the smell of freshly baked bread that suffused everything. She concentrated on negotiating the streets and was surprised to hear someone call her name. Inches from the car, so close she could have touched her, was Elena. There was a moment of stunned recognition, and then Elena was talking excitedly.

"You're back—that's super. Helmut was upset that you hadn't gotten in touch."

The traffic began to move and Elena ran a few steps with it. "I'll tell him I saw you. This time, phone."

"I'll try," Christa called back, smiling.

"Don't try—do it!" And then she was out of earshot.

A warm feeling of welcome softened the edges of Christa's tension. Looking around, she decided it felt good to be part of the comfortable bustle of the village. Then, before she was ready for it, the castle wall loomed on her right.

She pulled into the drive and parked her rented Opel behind Karl's Porsche. Her body suddenly ached with tension, but she forced herself to get out of the car, her legs unsteady. She should have called him or written, somehow found out what he was feeling. What if he hadn't missed her at all? Worse, what if he hated her for leaving? She looked at the castle but if she were searching for some sign of welcome, she was disappointed.

"Listen," she said to it, "if Karl still wants me I'm going to try my damnedest to get along well here, but you're going to have to help." She waited, half expecting an answer, but the castle was above her petty problems. Since his car was in the drive it was likely that Karl was on the grounds somewhere. She would try the yard first.

She followed the path behind the castle and pushed open the gate leading to the processing sheds. There was very little activity. The sheds themselves were empty, as were the stalls where the tractors were parked. As she crossed the dirt yard, someone came toward her from the back, where the gate opened onto the Bertastrasse. It was Edythe, approaching with a steady stride that never slowed, even when Christa could see by her eyes that she'd recognized her. She held her hands out and Christa grasped them. "My dear," Edythe said, a smile lighting up her face, "I can hardly believe it. Were you expected?"

"No."

"Karl doesn't know you're here?"

Christa shook her head. Edythe met her eyes in a long searching look that said more than words ever could. "I think he's in the vineyards, possibly in the hut at the top of the hill. Do you want me to send someone up to check?"

"No, thank you, I'd like to find him myself. How are things going? You look very busy."

"I am and it's wonderful. Things are going well, but I'm allowing myself to hope that your presence here means they will soon be even better. You will be with us for dinner?"

"I can't tell you that yet."

"I understand," Edythe said, "but I'll hope. If you won't be staying, please stop in the offices before you go. I'd like to visit with you for a bit."

"I will," Christa promised.

Edythe smiled again and touched her arm. "I'm so pleased to see you."

Christa left the yard and walked along the Berta-strasse. At the entrance to the vineyard she looked up, shading her eyes against the gray glare. The peak of the hut roof and the pennant fluttering in the breeze were visible, but because of the angle of the hill, she was unable to see if anyone was actually up there. Taking a deep breath and crossing both her fingers, she began to climb the steps. The air was heavy and a stiff breeze was blowing. The grape leaves moved against one another, and the immature grapes hung immobile—dusty, hard, round marbles of fruit—while the smell of rain permeated everything.

She counted the steps as she climbed in order to keep her mind off what she was doing. At twenty-five she stopped and looked up. Someone was watching from above. She lowered her head and went on. At fifty she stopped once more. Whoever it was she had seen, had seen her too and was standing at the edge of the dirt floor looking down at her intently. Her heart confirmed what her eyes still had trouble deciding—it was Karl. Resolutely she continued climbing. Thirty steps higher, she stopped again.

He had walked a few paces from the hut and was poised, bent slightly forward, watching her. The breeze lifted his hair, parting it. She thought he was more tanned than when she'd last seen him—at least his eyes seemed bluer. He had on a work shirt, open at the neck, and a pair of faded jeans. He took another step and hesitated.

How Christa's body sang at the sight of him; every muscle, every nerve was celebrating. For the first time in so long she felt like laughing, like shouting. She had more energy than she knew what to do with. Even over the distance that still separated them, the magic that existed between them was working. She could feel his response. "Hey," she called jubilantly, waving her arm at him, "remember me?"

He started toward her very slowly, like someone captured by a slow-motion camera. Then, as he became convinced that what he saw was real, he ran the rest of the way down to her. She opened her arms wide in welcome and he lifted her off her feet, his arms tight around her, his lips crushing hers. Clinging to the familiar warm strength of him, Christa knew she'd really come home. She was where she belonged.

She touched his face lightly and he drew back to look at her. "I've never been as angry with another human being as I am with you," he said, and kissed her roughly again. "How the hell could you have done that to me? To us?"

She stood on tiptoe and silenced him with her lips. His hands on her back were strong and possessive. The first drops of rain spattered the dust at their feet.

"We'll have to get out of here," Karl said, "these steps are impassable when they're wet." He hurried her off the mountain and into a small office in the processing yard, closing the door on what had become a downpour. Her dress was splotched with raindrops and beads of water clung to the fine hairs on Karl's arms. He stood with his back to the door watching her. "You damn near killed me," he told her, "running away like that."

"I didn't run away." She faced him for a moment, and then dropped her gaze. "I guess I *was* running away. But there was so much involved, Karl, so many problems, and I couldn't see my way around them."

"And do you see your way around them now?"

She looked out the window at the rain and shook her head. "Not really."

"Then why did you come back?"

"Because I love you and maybe you were right. Maybe it will be enough. I hope so, because I found out that without it nothing else has any meaning either." He crossed the room slowly and pulled her against him so that her head rested on his chest. "All the things I didn't want to give up were right where I left them, Karl, and I was miserable. I guess I want it all. I want you *and* what I left behind, but I know I can't have that. Some of it I can replace, but not you. So I came back."

"*Liebchen*," he whispered, his mouth against her hair.

"I loved you the first time I saw you, and I love you still. Is that going to be enough to solve our problems?"

He tipped her head up and kissed her tenderly. "I promise you, it will be."

"I'll never wear a black cardigan," she said softly, "and I won't compete with Edythe for the winery, and I can't just be your shadow." She looked up at him. "I'll need something for myself."

"I know. I really do. The deepest part of me knows what it is you're giving up for me, and I ache that you have to do it and feel joy that you will. I've experienced a lot of emotions in my life—anger, loneliness, frustration, hate—but it took you to introduce me to fear. You had ten days left before I came to Boston to get you."

"In ten days there wouldn't have been much of me left to get."

He moved away from her slightly so that he could look clearly into her eyes. "Don't ever leave me again."

"I won't," she promised, shaken by the intensity of what she saw there. "You're my sweet destiny, and I'm yours forever." Then, cuddling once more against him, a small smile touched her lips. "All the pieces are back together again."

Karl looked at her questioningly.

"My mizpah coin," she explained. "It's all one piece again—a perfect fit."

"Not as perfect as this," Karl said, bringing his lips to hers.

"No," she agreed. "Nothing is as perfect as this."

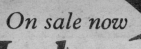